BEFORE

Praise for Before The Mast:

'This is the perfect Lockdown novel. A page turner that will have you laughing, crying and sitting on the edge of your seat. Beautifully written, sharp, witty, poignant, historically accurate but with real heart at the centre. Can't wait to read the next installation.'
Siobhan Rowden, author of Stardust Academy.

'Oh wow what a rip-roaring yarn of a tale! I thoroughly enjoyed this book from start to end, it never let up in the flow of the story at all. It gets gruesome and very dark in some places but wow I honestly couldn't put it down! This is such a good book and told from an accurate point of view, and I love the ending. I honestly cannot wait for more from this author!'
Lil-monster, reviewer.

'Really well written, the story is at times dark but combined with such funny moments. Excited that there is sequel coming, I need to know what happens next!'
JayM, reviewer.

'Good old fashioned ripping yarn. What a belter.'
Nico, reviewer.

The Adventures of Dan Leake

BEFORE THE MAST

J.R. MULHOLLAND

J.R. Mulholland   Chesterfield

1. Edition, 2021

While some of the events and characters are based
on historical incidents and figures, this novel is
entirely a work of fiction.

For LH Sasha Fierce,

the Royal Navy's finest.

.

CONTENTS

CHAPTER 1

MAN-O-WAR

A cold November wind sliced across the water and cut into the dockside. Dan Leake shivered, a thin cotton shirt and torn breeches his only protection from the biting cold. He pulled his top closer around him as he looked eagerly at the ships bobbing in Bristol harbour. Merchantmen of all shapes and sizes lay at anchor - sloops, barques and brigs - but his keen gaze quickly settled on the man-o-war. It was 1719, and Britain was at war with Spain, so the big ship bustled with activity as men toiled to haul ammunition and provisions up the sloping gangplank.

The *Dover* dwarfed the surrounding vessels, though his friend Tom had told him it wasn't even a first-rate ship-of the-line. Tom knew about these things. His father had been in the Royal Navy. So had Dan's, but Tom's dad had come home. Dan's never had.

He'd only been six when his father had been pressed into the navy, eight long years before. His mother said he'd had been too drunk to run when the press-gang raided the tavern in their home town of Cork, but Dan didn't believe her. *His dad wasn't a drunk, and anyway, he wouldn't have run.* They had neither seen nor heard from him since.

All this time Dan had been waiting for his father to come home, but he could wait no longer. His mother, despairing of her husband ever returning, had moved them to her sister's house in Bristol, hoping for a better life. But now his mother and aunt lay dead, killed by the fever that had swept through the slums of Blackboy Hill that summer. If Dan stayed then he'd be picked up and put in the workhouse, if he didn't starve first.

No, if his dad couldn't come to him then he'd go to his dad. He was going to run away to sea, and he'd persuaded his friend Tom to go with him. They'd decided to meet here at ten o'clock, but Tom was late.

He heard footsteps behind him and turned, smiling, just as a stone whistled past his ear.

"Oi! Bog trotter! I told you to stay away from here. Get back to your slum."

Billy Mellor, a hulking brute a couple of years older than Dan, treated him to a mirthless smile. He had two of his mates with him, and they grinned as the smaller boy took a faltering step back.

Despite the cold, Dan could feel sweat beading on his forehead. He could taste the salt as it dripped down to his dry lips. He struggled to control his laboured breathing as the boys spread out around him. *I'm in big trouble unless Tom gets here fast.*

His eyes darted around, searching for an escape route, but there was none to be seen. They would catch him before he could dodge into the bustling maze of the marketplace. He swallowed hard. It wouldn't be the first time he'd had a beating from Billy and his gang, and he felt the cold fingers of despair clawing into his chest.

They closed in.

"I hear your no-good mother's gone the same way as your non-existent father," Billy sneered, swaggering towards him with all the confidence of his superior size and years.

The laughter of the bully's side-kicks rang in Dan's ears, growing louder and louder until it filled his head with its clamour. His hands slowly clenched, a red mist coming down over his eyes. Billy took one more step, and Dan launched himself forward, fists flying.

Billy staggered back, the unexpected attack throwing him off balance. "Get him!" he yelled to his mates as he tripped and fell backwards, but they stood, frozen to the spot.

Dan was on him in a second, pinning him down, all the anger, sorrow and fear of the last months flowing into his fists as he smashed them down, again and again.

Strong arms pulled him off his squealing victim. He bucked and fought, thinking that Billy's pals had finally joined in.

"Dan! Dan! It's me!" The sound of Tom's deep voice slowly sank in and he stopped struggling, all the energy draining out of him along with the anger.

"Bloody hell, Dan! You've made a right mess of him!" A sudden grin lit up Tom's round face. "Good man!"

Dan looked down.

Billy Mellor lay snivelling, blood seeping from his

3

squashed nose and cut lips. "Keep him away from me," he squealed as he squirmed away on his back. "He's a bloody nutter!"

"Shut your mouth, Mellor," growled Tom, "or you'll get a boot up the arse from me as well."

Billy struggled to his feet, face contorted, about to say something. Tom took a step towards him, and he turned tail and ran. Tom sent a stone skimming after him to help him on his way.

"Where are the other two?" panted Dan, pulling in great lungfuls of air. "There were three of them."

"The cowards ran off when they saw me coming."

There was no mistaking the edge of disappointment in Tom's voice. He was the same age as Dan but was already bigger than Billy Mellor, and he loved a scrap.

He slapped Dan on the back. "I didn't know you had it in you, mate. That was awesome. Where did that come from?"

"He was on about my mum and dad. He just made me mad, that's all."

"Well remind me never to make you mad then. Awesome!" He slapped Dan on the back again before leading him over to the harbour wall.

They stared at the hulking warship, eyes wide with excitement. Tom had always wanted to join the Royal Navy, but his mum wouldn't let him. His dad had been full of stories about battles and wild adventures, but then for days at a time he'd sit in brooding silence, gazing blankly back into the past. His mum would just shake her head and warn Tom not to join up.

Something on the ship caught Dan's eye. It was a long, white dress, and in it was the most beautiful girl he'd ever seen. He watched, fascinated, as she sauntered around the deck. She stopped occasionally to toss back her long, blonde hair, or exchange a few words with the sailors who all touched a forelock deferentially when she spoke to them. A slow smile spread across Dan's face.

"She's magnificent isn't she?" came Tom's awed voice.

"Yes. Beautiful."

"Look at the rigging on her!"

Dan didn't like the way the conversation was going, but he nodded. "Aye, very nice."

"And she's seen plenty of action too."

Dan turned on his friend, fists bunched. "You don't even know her!" he yelled.

Tom took a step back, eyes wide and mouth working silently. "I kn-know all about her," he stammered. "She's the *Dover*. Saw action at the Battle of Solebay. She's a 50 gunner. Six hundred tons. Crew of..."

"Oh! The ship?"

"Of course, 'the ship'. What did you think I was talking about?" Tom turned back just in time to see a white dress disappearing into the grand cabin. "Oh! I see!"

He started laughing, great belly laughs from deep inside, his shock of blond hair bobbing about as he rocked back and forward holding his sides.

Dan scowled at him, feeling foolish, but then the corners of his mouth began to turn up into a grin. He started to laugh, gently at first but then louder and louder until they were both rolling on the ground, tears streaming down their dirt-smeared faces.

Tom smiled as they climbed to their feet and dusted themselves down. "Talking of the ship, have you thought about how we can get on board?"

"We're at war with Spain. The navy will be after men and boys. We can walk straight up the gangplank. I'm sure we'll be welcomed with open arms." Dan smiled. "And I've heard there might be a cash bounty for signing on as volunteers."

Tom wasn't so sure. "You may be right, but they might contact my parents, and Ma would be bound to stop me. Better to sneak on board after it's dark. The ship will be sailing on the morning tide, and they'll not turn back once they find us."

Nodding his agreement, Dan looked thoughtfully at his friend. This had been his idea and he now felt guilty for dragging him into it, just because he hadn't the courage to do it alone.

"Are you sure you want to go through with this, Tom? Your mum's going to miss you, isn't she?"

Tom's eyes moistened a little, but his voice was steady when he spoke. "Ma's got nine others to fret about. One less mouth to feed is one less worry for her, and besides," he clapped Dan on the back again, "I'm not having you running off and having all the fun without me. Who'd look out for you?"

They gazed at the D*over* one more time, and then arranged to meet again at dusk. When their adventure would begin for real.

CHAPTER 2

STOWAWAY

The wind had dropped, but so had the temperature. Dan waited, huddled against the chill stone of the harbour wall. Tom was late. Tom was always late. *Tonight of all nights!* He reached into his pocket and pulled out a well-worn silver locket, the only thing of value that he owned. *But he would never sell it, no matter how hungry he was.*

Hands fumbling in the cold, he found the catch and opened it. He gazed fondly at the fading portrait inside. A dark-haired man with a square chin and a broken nose, stared back at him. A hard face, but softened by a smiling pair of twinkling blue eyes. His father. The locket had been a gift to his wife in better times, before the press-gang had taken him.

A rustling sound spun Dan around and there was Tom.

"Early again, I see," Tom teased him.

Dan snapped the locket shut and stuffed it into the breast pocket of his shirt. He turned and looked at the ship. He could sense rather than see the grin on Tom's big, round face. He couldn't stay mad at him.

"Yeah! That's it. I'm early again."

"What's going on down there?" asked Tom.

Dan could hear the suppressed excitement quivering in the loud attempt at a whisper. "The ship's quiet," he said, "except for a couple of marines guarding the gangplank. But they'll be looking for people sneaking off, not sneaking on."

"We should swim around to the other side and climb on where they can't see us," said Tom.

"In this weather? Are you mad? We could be hiding out for days before they find us. We'd freeze to death if we got a soaking."

"What's your plan then, brain-box?" A sullen edge had crept into Tom's voice. He was an expert at the one-second sulk, but his cheerful nature wouldn't allow him to carry on for any longer than that.

"See that hawser at the bow? It's out of sight of the guards and it's close to that jollyboat on deck. We can shin up it and hide out in the boat until the ship sets sail. They'll not spot us in the dark."

Tom's enthusiasm was back straight away. "Let's go then!"

"Wait!" Dan placed a restraining hand on his friend's arm. "Have you brought any food?"

Tom produced a loaf of bread and some cheese. "How about you?"

Dan shook his head. "Sorry, I couldn't get anything." He hadn't eaten for two days, and he stared hungrily at the bread. His stomach rumbled, but he resisted the temptation to eat straight away.

Tom touched his arm. "Come on, I'll race you."

"Don't be stupid, we've got to... Tom... Tom!" But his friend was already halfway down to the moored ship.

As Dan reached the bottom of the stone steps he found Tom squinting around the corner of the wall.

"It's all clear," Tom whispered like a foghorn, "Do you want to go first or shall I?"

Dan held back. Butterflies fluttered in his stomach, but he didn't want Tom to know he was scared. "I'll go firs... Tom... Tom!"

His friend had already reached the hawser that tied the bow of the ship to the wharf. Slowly shaking his head, Dan crouched down and hurried after him.

By the time Dan got to the hawser, Tom had nearly reached the top, squirming up the thick rope like a monkey. Dan gingerly took hold of it then wrapped his arms and legs around tightly. Slowly he inched his way up. He hated heights.

Suddenly the hawser started swaying crazily. He clung on, eyes darting about in panic. They finally focused on Tom at the ships rail, grinning away and swinging the rope for all he was worth.

"Stop it you idiot," he called as loudly as he dared.

Tom's smiling face disappeared behind the bulwark and the rope steadied. Heart pounding, Dan pulled himself up and clambered over the rail. He lay there, gulping in lungfuls of air.

Tom appeared beside him. "Come on, I've found us a good hidey-hole."

It was the boat that Dan had spotted from the dock. The covering tarpaulin would protect them from wind, rain, and prying eyes. They lifted the tarp and scrambled in, falling in a heap at the bottom.

"I've found us the perfect spot, haven't I?" crowed Tom. "It's a good job you've got me looking after you, Danny boy."

"But it was my ide–"

"Have some cheese," Tom interrupted, passing over a rancid-smelling slice, and a hunk of stale bread as well.

Immediately forgetting his grievance, Dan wolfed down the food.

With something in his belly, a sudden drowsiness came over him. It had been a long day and he felt his eyes slowly closing.

"We'd better get some sleep, Tom. We don't know what tomorrow has in store for us."

"I'm too excited to sleep," yawned Tom, stretching his arms wide. "You get your head down. I'll keep first watch."

Within minutes, Dan could hear his friend snoring. He smiled to himself as he curled up in the corner. He was warm, his belly was full, and he was going to find his dad. *Everything was going to be alright.* He drifted off into a deep, contented sleep, and dreamt of ships, sea battles, and a girl in a white dress.

Dan awoke with a start. A sudden panic clawed at his stomach as the very ground swayed beneath him. Then he heard Tom's snores and remembered where he was. His heart raced. They were under way.

He reached up and pulled back the tarpaulin, cautiously

poking his head out. Wide-eyed he looked around taking everything in: the sails billowing in the wind, men scampering about in the rigging, officers shouting orders, the whole ship alive and bustling. He nudged his friend awake with his foot.

"Give me another hour Mum, I'm tired."

"I'm not your ruddy mother," snapped Dan.

Tom sat up, rubbing his eyes. "Where are... Oh yeah, I remember."

Dan crouched down beside him. "We're out of sight of land. Shall we go and see the captain?"

Tom thought for a minute, which surprised Dan. "We should wait a bit longer. We don't want them putting us on a passing ship heading back into port. Oh, and another thing." Tom stretched and yawned before carrying on. "We should give false names and tell the captain we're orphans. That way he'll not get any ideas that we should be back home with our mums. Oh! Sorry, Dan."

Dan swallowed hard. "That's okay. It's a good idea." But then something occurred to him. "How am I supposed to find my dad if I don't say who I am?"

"Alright, we'll give our names," conceded Tom.

Dan scratched his head. "And I think–"

As he spoke, a huge, hairy fist thrust under the tarpaulin, grabbed him by the collar and yanked him out of the boat.

"A stowaway, eh?" An evil looking man with a barrel chest and thick, hairy arms pushed his stubbly face close to Dan's. He could smell the rum on the sailor's rancid breath. "What should I do with ye? Take ye to the cap'n or just throw ye overboard?"

11

"I'd rather go to the captain, sir."

The man glared, fist raised, trying to work out if Dan was making fun of him or not.

Just then Tom's head popped up from the jollyboat. "Morning," he said cheerfully. "I'm Tom."

The sailor exploded. "How many more of you little buggers are in there?"

"Just me," smiled Tom, clambering out to join Dan.

The man stormed over to the boat and stuck his grizzled head under the tarpaulin. Satisfied there was no one else there, he turned on the boys.

"I'm the bosun on this here vessel, and don't forget it." He puffed out his chest. "Follow me."

He strode off towards the stern of the ship, a wicked-looking knotted rope swinging in his right hand. Dan gulped and glanced at Tom who gave him a reassuring smile, and they fell into step behind the burly seaman.

Commodore Philip Cavendish looked up from an ornate wooden desk, pushing a well-thumbed book aside. "What have we here, Mr Savage? Volunteers? That's a rarity these days."

"They're stinking stowaways, Cap'n. Shall I put them on punishment duties?"

"Of course not, Mr Savage. They're volunteers." He smiled and winked at the boys. "You *are* volunteers, aren't you lads?"

His smile was infectious and they grinned back.

"Yes, sir," they replied together.

Behind them, the bosun scowled and slapped the

knotted rope into his own thigh.

"It's a shame you didn't sign on before we sailed," said the captain. "You'd have had a nice bounty payment tucked away in your purses, and a mug of rum warming your bellies."

Dan's smile dropped and he threw his friend an 'I told you so' look, but Tom only shrugged.

"But as you miraculously appeared at sea, I'm afraid there will be no bounty. You can sign on as volunteers, or I can list you as pressed men. I leave it up to you."

"We'll volunteer, sir," said Tom. Dan nodded his agreement.

"Good lads." Commodore Cavendish entered the date, *14th November 1719*, into the ship's log. "Do your parents know that you're at sea?"

"We're orphans, sir." Again Tom spoke before Dan had the chance.

The captain's face darkened. "Orphans eh? I don't like orphans. The damned orphanages teach you to read and write, and then you start thinking you're better than you are. It makes a boy uppity."

"We're not from an orphanage," Dan piped up. "We fended for ourselves."

"You did, did you? So you're thieves. Thieves, beggars and scroungers." The captain's smile was bright and sudden. "Excellent! Give me a thief any day, rather than an urchin who can read and write."

Dan's mother had taught him to read and write back in Ireland, and he'd even been to school a few times, but he decided that it might be a good idea to keep that to himself.

"I'll have no stealing on this ship, mind. I'll have the skin off the back of any man I catch thieving, and you'll get worse from your shipmates. Many a thief has disappeared overboard on a dark night. At best they'll have you run the gauntlet, as each man lashes you bloody. Do you understand me?"

"Yes, sir," said Tom.

"No stealing," said Dan.

Philip Cavendish studied the slight, black-haired boy in front of him. Small, all skin and bone, but with piercing blue eyes that didn't waver as he regarded him.

"You'll make a good powder monkey. We need plenty of those. They're always blowing themselves up."

Dan turned pale.

"You're a bit scrawny, but we'll soon feed you up. The food's horrible, but there's plenty of it." The captain laughed and turned to Tom who was staring out of the stern window, watching seagulls squabbling over scraps of food. He noted that the youngster was nearly as tall as the brawny bosun. "How old are you, boy?"

Tom came out of his daydream. "How old am I? Nearly fifteen, sir. Same as Dan. We were born on the same day."

"You don't look like twins to me."

"We're not, sir. We–."

"I know you're not. Permit me to have a bit of levity now and then."

Tom cast a worried glance at Dan, unsure what he was permitting the captain to have a bit of.

"You're a big lad for fourteen. A bit big for a powder monkey. We might make a sailor out of you. Have you

14

any experience of the sea?"

"No, sir, but I know about ships. My father was in the Royal Navy. Rated able seaman."

"Was he indeed? Well we'll start you as a powder monkey and see how you go on. Now, let's get you signed up. What are your names?"

"Tom Bailey, sir."

"Tommm Baaaillleey!" The captain drawled out the name as he noted it in the ship's log. He looked up at Dan. "And you?"

"Dan Leake, sir."

"Leak? I don't want any leaks in my ship," roared the captain, then laughed at his own witticism.

"Leake with an 'e', sir."

The laughter stopped. "So you can spell, can you?"

"No, sir," Dan lied quickly, "but my dad always said it was Leake with an 'e'."

"And where is your father now, Master Leake?"

"Gone, sir."

"Gone? Gone where?"

Dan wasn't yet ready to ask about his dad. It didn't seem to be the right time.

Noticing the young man's reluctance to answer, the captain held up a hand. "Gone to the Devil, for all I care. As long as you obey the rules, do your duty, and kill Spaniards, I'll be happy."

He pushed the ship's log across the table, dipped his quill in an ink pot and handed it to Tom who made his mark, a cross with a circle around it. Tom passed the quill to Dan who began to sign his name. Tom elbowed him in the ribs, and Dan hastily put a diagonal slash through the 'D' that he'd written.

The captain took the log and looked suspiciously at Dan. 'Dan Leake. Fourteen. Dark hair, blue eyes,' he wrote next to Dan's mark. 'Tom Bailey. Fourteen. Blond hair, blue eyes,' he noted by Tom's squiggle. "Any distinguishing marks or tattoos?"

"I've got a birthmark on my back, sir," said Dan before Tom could stop him. The Royal Navy recorded this information to help them to track down deserters.

"Let's see it then, Leake. Let's see it."

Dan lifted his threadbare shirt and showed the oval birthmark, high on the right side of his back. The captain noticed the protruding ribs as he recorded the information.

"Addresses? No, of course not!"

He turned to the glowering bosun. "Mr Savage! Put Master Leake in the starboard watch, under the tender care of, Scar."

"Aye Aye, sir."

The bosun gave Dan an evil smirk. "Scar will soon sort you out," he muttered.

Dan's knees went weak. *Who was Scar?*

"And put Master Bailey in the larboard watch, under Sam Kelly."

Tom spoke up straight away. "I want to be with Dan."

The bosun's knotted rope came down hard on Tom's back. "You don't question orders!" he roared.

Tom's fists clenched and Dan prayed he wouldn't do anything stupid. His friend's fingers slowly straightened, and Dan let out a sigh of relief.

The captain paid no attention to the casual violence. "And teach them how to salute an officer. We don't want to see them flogged on their first day, do we?"

"No, sir," said the bosun, while his scowling face said the opposite.

"Oh, and Mister Savage?" Commodore Cavendish looked again at Dan's thin frame. "Make sure that these fine young volunteers have something to eat before you put them to work."

"Aye Aye, sir."

The bosun marched them out of the cabin and down to the ship's galley.

The warmth in the galley was nearly as wonderful as having a belly full of food — salt beef in a thick pea soup. Dan couldn't remember the last time he'd had a hot meal. They each had a chunk of bread to go with it, and they were now greedily mopping up the remains of the broth in their wooden bowls.

The cook was a portly man with a patch over one eye. He had moaned that breakfast had finished an hour before, but he turned out to be kindly enough and had even given them second helpings. He waddled over to them, squeezing in his stomach as he sidled down the narrow gangway. He held out his one hand to collect their bowls. The other was missing at the wrist, the arm ending with a hook set in a leather-covered stump. He noticed Dan staring at it.

"Lost it at Beachy Head, back in 'oh seven'," he said proudly. "Now *that* was a battle. Outnumbered four to one, we were."

"And what about your eye?" asked Tom.

"Now there's a sad tale." The jowls on the cook's chubby face quivered as he spoke, and a tear formed in his one good eye. "I got a grain of sand in it."

"A grain of sand?" Tom raised an eyebrow. "How did you lose your eye to a grain of sand?"

"It was my first day with the hook. I forgot that I had it," laughed the cook. "Well gentlemen, have you had enough?"

Dan grinned and amazed himself by saying yes, and actually meaning it. Tom, of course, wanted more.

"That's a shame," said the cook. "Because there isn't any more. Now get yourselves up on deck and report to Mister Savage."

Dan started to fret again now that their little moment of heaven was over. It was bad enough having to report to the brute of a bosun, but what really worried him was the name that kept jumping, unbidden, into his head. *Scar!* He'd tried to find out about him from the cook, but when he told him he'd be working with Scar, the man had just said 'Oh dear!' and given him second helpings.

He'd also asked about the girl in the white dress. She was the captain's niece, and he was taking her as far as Lisbon in Portugal where she was at finishing school. 'Don't even think about it,' the cook had warned him, but Dan could think of little else. Until the thought of Scar chased her from his mind.

They reached the hatch and climbed out into the bright November sunshine. In front of them, on their hands and knees, men scrubbed the deck and swabbed it with rope yarn. Others could be seen high in the rigging making small adjustments to the sails. Yet more stood by the guns lining either side of the deck.

The bosun lurked by the foot of the quarterdeck, talking to the tall marine guarding the stairwell. He spotted the boys and rounded on them.

"About time," he snapped. "Have you eaten the whole ship's rations? Come with me."

He marched them over to the larboard guns, stopping by a small, friendly-looking man dressed in a striped shirt and pantaloons. Like most of the seamen, his feet were bare.

"Got a new powder monkey for ye, Kelly."

Sam Kelly glanced up at Tom who was a head taller than him. "Looks more like a powder bleeding elephant to me. What have you been feeding him on?"

"This is Sam Kelly, yer gun-captain," the bosun growled at Tom. "Learn from him and do what yer told, or ye'll feel the end o' my rope!" He then walked away with Dan, who suddenly felt very small and alone.

The bosun stopped in the middle of the deck, looking at the starboard gun-crews who stood by their cannons, ready for the morning's gunnery practise.

"Guess which one's your mate Scar."

Dan looked over at the waiting men. Several of them were scarred and most of them had an aura of violence about them, but one stood out. Head and shoulders above the others, bare-chested showing a heavily muscled body, with a vivid scar running from his left ear to his chin, towered a giant black man.

He had never seen anyone of that colour before, and he stared, open-mouthed. The huge man returned his look with narrowed, malevolent eyes that seemed to bore hatred into his skull.

The bosun followed Dan's terrified gaze and he gave an evil grin. He put his mouth to Dan's ear and whispered, "Come and meet Scar."

CHAPTER 3

SCAR

The bosun dragged Dan over to the waiting gun-crew and shoved him towards the huge man at their head. "Got a new powder monkey for ye, Scar. Try to keep him alive a bit longer than the last one."

He turned to Dan.

"Do what Scar tells ye now, not that he'll tell ye a lot."

He laughed then stomped off, swinging his knotted rope at a loitering boy.

Scar scowled down at Dan who stared back defiantly, trying not show his fear, his eyes straying to the dreadful wound on the man's face. A hand the size of a shovel took him by the shoulder, spun him around and propelled him across the deck to an open hatchway. Scar pointed to it and Dan clambered down. Two more flights of steps followed, the light growing dimmer and dimmer as they descended into the bowels of the ship.

Dan found himself in front of a covered doorway guarded by a marine who quickly stepped back when Scar appeared. The big man pulled the heavy curtain aside and pushed Dan forward. Stairs led down into a pitch-black void. Dan took a tentative step before another push sent him half-stumbling to the bottom. He crouched there, sweat running down his neck, his hands clammy but cold. No torches or lanterns burned on the walls. The darkness complete.

Heavy footsteps sounded on the stairs, coming slowly but steadily down towards him. He could hear the steps groaning and straining, but could see nothing. He screwed his eyes closed, trying to shut out the darkness.

He jumped as a huge hand clamped around his arm, dragging him across the room then forcing him to his knees. His pulse thumped in his temples, his breath coming in laboured rasps as he waited — *for what*?

As his eyes adjusted to the darkness, Dan could just make out the outline of the giant man who mimed picking something from the floor, putting it into a canister, then sealing it. He passed the container to Dan who bent down and scrabbled about beneath him. He could feel a number of canvas bags around him. Hoping he'd guessed right he picked one up, placed it in the canister then shut the lid. He stood up. Scar pushed him back to the stairs, and they climbed out past the guard, clambered up to the hatchway and out into welcome daylight.

They made their way across the deck to where several men waited by the gun. Scar pointed to a sailor by the mouth of the cannon and Dan undid the container and passed him the cartridge. Scar nodded then shoved him towards the hatch again. Dan understood and scampered off for more gunpowder.

He was now a fully trained powder monkey.

"It's a piece of cake, isn't it?" said Tom, wolfing down a bowl of burgoo. "Nothing to it."

Dan gave a hesitant nod. He picked at the boiled oatmeal, and took a sip of watered-down rum.

"I'm thinking they'll be wanting more from us than just fetching powder. I'm not looking forward to going up in the rigging."

A vision of the towering mainmast, popped into his head and a shudder went through him.

"You'll be fine," said Tom, staring thirstily at Dan's almost full mug. "Are you gonna drink that?"

Dan pushed it over to him. "You'd better take it easy with that, Tom. It's strong stuff."

"I'm sound," he slurred, downing the drink and burping loudly before looking thoughtfully at Dan. "What's Scar like then? Is he as mean as they say he is?"

"I don't know. He hasn't spoken a word to me yet."

"And he's not likely to either," said Sam Kelly as he got up from the table. "Scar's a mute."

As they took in this information, the bosun swaggered towards them, ducking down under the low beams overhead.

"What are ye doing at that table, Leake? Yer supposed to eat with yer own gun-crew."

"I was just—"

"Never mind what ye were just doing. Report to the quartermaster, the pair of ye."

A few minutes later they were staring blankly at lengths of cloth, scissors, needles and thread. They looked at the material, at each other, then back at the quartermaster.

"Well," he said, "what are you waiting for? Stop swinging the lead. Get on with it!"

"Get on with what, sir?" asked Dan.

"Make and mend. Tidy up those rags that you're wearing, and sew new jackets and trousers for yourselves."

"But we don't know how to make clothes," complained Tom.

"Then you're going to have some cold, miserable times ahead of you. Now shove off, the pair of you."

Behind them a pimply, weasel-like boy sniggered.

Tom whirled around. "Shut your gob, you corn-faced beau-nasty."

The skinny boy backed away, but his lip curled and his shifty eyes followed them as Dan and Tom moved to the companionway.

"Who was that?" asked Dan.

"Henry Hall. He's powder monkey on the gun next to mine. London pickpocket. Chose the navy rather than prison. Don't leave your purse open when he's around."

"What purse?" moaned Dan. "Even if I had one, I'd have nothing to put in it."

"Don't trust him, that's all."

Up on deck they laid out the cloth and studied it doubtfully. Tom's face scrunched up as he concentrated, trying to work out where to start. He suddenly brightened then set to, cutting and sewing with wild abandon. Dan watched his efforts in silence.

"Piece of cake," said Tom, smiling at his completed handiwork.

"Looks more like a piece of cack," laughed Dan. "Try them on then."

Tom pulled on his new jacket. It barely came down to his bellybutton and the sleeves were halfway up his arms. He struggled into the trousers.

"They're never going to fit, mate. Not in a million years."

"Yes they are," panted Tom, his face contorted as he heaved the trousers up over his muscular thighs. "There," he cried in triumph. "Perfect fit."

As he bent down to pick up his needle and thread there was a loud ripping sound, and Tom's hairy arse appeared through a large split in his trousers.

"Maybe they could do with a couple of adjustments here and there," he laughed.

As Tom sewed a new panel into the seat of his pants, Dan studied the cloth in front of him. He didn't want to make the same mistakes as his friend. As he pondered, he noticed Lieutenant Trimble's dog stop behind Tom. It squatted and deposited a steaming pile on the deck before racing off to chase the ship's monkey into the rigging. The monkey stopped in the safety of the ropes, screeching defiance at the barking dog. The sailors grinned and egged it on. They regarded the monkey as *their* pet whereas the dog belonged to a lieutenant, therefore any small victory for the monkey over the dog was a victory for them over the officers.

"There," said Tom, pulling on his trousers again. "What do you think of that?"

He stepped back to allow Dan to admire his handiwork,

and stood straight in the dog mess.

"Oh! For the love of…"

He bent down and wiped the foul-smelling muck off his bare foot with a spare piece of cloth, as Dan rolled around laughing.

The bosun marched over.

"What are you two larking about at? You're supposed to be working!"

As he spoke he stepped in the oozing pile. His foot shot out from under him, and he crashed to the deck.

"I did that," said Tom.

"Ye did, did ye, ye dirty bugger," yelled the bosun, jumping up and swiping at Tom with his knotted rope. "In future use the toilets like everyone else. Now get that mess cleaned up."

With a final swipe of the rope he turned and squelched off up the deck.

Dan's shoulders shook as he tried to keep himself from laughing. "Are you all right, mate?"

Tom chuckled then groaned, holding his back where the rope had hit him, then chuckled again. Then they were both off, laughing until they cried.

When he'd got his breath back, Dan went to see the cook and returned with a piece of charcoal. Holding the cloth up against himself, he used the charcoal to carefully mark the lengths and sizes he wanted. Once it was marked out, he cut along the lines and then started to sew.

Tom looked on doubtfully.

Slowly but surely two items of clothing appeared. Dan took off his old, torn trousers and tried on the new ones.

"Those are a smashing pair of farting-crackers," admitted Tom. "Try on the jacket."

Compared to Tom's effort, the baggy, ill-fitting rag could have been made by a professional tailor.

"Beginner's luck," growled Tom, punching Dan playfully on the arm.

He looked down uncertainly at his own clothes.

"I think mine might be a bit tight."

"Don't worry," grinned Dan. "You'll grow into them."

CHAPTER 4

RACE TO THE TOPS

It being the Sabbath, most of the crew relaxed on deck after Sunday service, leaving an unfortunate few to sail the ship. Sam Kelly called them over.

"Dan! Tom! Come with me. I've been told to show you the ropes. We'll start at the prow and work our way back and down."

He took them to the bow and pointed out the heads - four rough holes cut into wooden planks suspended over the water.

"This is where you go to the toilet. Make sure you hold on tight when the wind's blowing. We've lost a few young lads that way. The captain hates writing to their mothers. 'Died heroically in battle,' has a better ring to it than, 'Fell overboard while having a poo.' So make sure that you take a good grip."

Tom paled. "Good grip, safe shit," he repeated to himself, over and over again.

"This is the tow rag."

Sam Kelly pulled up a rope with a cloth tied to the end that had been floating in the sea.

"For wiping your bum," he added when he saw the boys' blank expressions.

Dan stared open-mouthed at the filth-encrusted rag.

"I don't think I'll be using that," he muttered to Tom, whose face was screwed up in horror.

"I'm not taking a dump until we get back to shore," swore Tom.

Sam kicked a trough-like urinal mounted on the bulkhead and draining into the scuppers. "Those are the pissdales. One on either side of the ship so you don't have to piss into the wind. Always go on the lee side if you don't want it blowing back in your face."

Again the boys looked less than impressed.

"There's no privacy aboard a ship," said Sam, seeing the look they exchanged, "so get used to it. Anyway, that's the bowsprit. That's the jib. That's the fore topmast staysail. That's the..."

As Sam droned on, Dan found his mind wandering. *How was he going to find his Dad? The captain would know how to trace him. He'd speak with him the next chance he got.* His face lit up at the thought.

"This is the fo'c'sle, where the hands sleep, and gather when off-duty. This is where you stow your..."

Dan frowned. *Would he even recognise his dad when he saw him? He had the locket but it had been eight years.* He tried to picture him in his head. *Short black hair. Blue eyes. An occasional stubbly beard that scratched when he played with him. A big man, five foot eleven tall, fully six inches above average height. Burly, with a square jaw and a nose flattened in some past brawl.*

He remembered that his dad liked a fight and the locals would keep out of his way when he'd been drinking and had the temper on him. But he had laughing blue eyes that softened his face, and he had never raised a hand to Dan or his mother.

"That's the quarterdeck. You only go up there if you're ordered or invited — unless you want a flogging. That's the mizzen mast. This is the…"

Sam gabbled on until they finally reached the bottom of the ship.

"And these are the bilges."

The stink physically stung Dan's eyes, and he could hear Tom gagging.

Sam seemed quite at home.

"Ships are made of wood and they leak. The water has to be pumped out. It gets worse in bad weather when the timbers are straining then sometimes it's all hands to the pumps to keep the ship afloat. It's hard graft so the pumps are worked from the deck where the men can breathe."

"Why does it smell so bad?" gasped Tom, holding his nose and looking askance at the foul liquid washing around his bare feet.

"Partly because it's stagnant," said Sam, "and partly because the lazy swabs working down here can't be bothered with the long climb up to the heads. So they just do their business here in the bilges."

Tom seemed to hover as he tried to lift both feet out of the water at the same time.

Soon afterwards they were back topside and breathing clean air. Sam Kelly left them practising rope-splicing as he strolled off to smoke his pipe and laze around with the other off-duty sailors.

Unused to life at sea, Dan's soft hands were beginning to hurt so he took a rest from splicing, his thoughts again turning to his father. He pulled out the silver locket as Henry Hall slouched by, his shifty eyes missing nothing. Dan noticed the sly look, and made a mental note to be more careful in future. The simple locket was a thing of value in this company. As he went to return it to his pocket, the cabin door opened and Dan found himself looking at a dainty pair of feet. He caught a flash of ankle then noticed the familiar white dress. He raised his head and stared, open-mouthed.

She was even more beautiful close up. Her long, golden hair framed a high cheek-boned, oval face with full red lips, a pert nose and a pair of striking green, almond-shaped eyes. But it was her skin that fascinated him most. It was the smoothest skin that he'd ever seen, unmarked by smallpox or other illness. His heart jumped and butterflies played in his stomach. He tried to catch her eye, but she looked straight through him. As she turned to the steps of the quarterdeck though, she threw Tom a quick smile.

Dan glowered at his friend as the girl disappeared up the companionway.

"What?" said Tom, "It's not my fault if I'm irresistible to women, is it?"

He laughed but Dan didn't.

"There's plenty more fish in the sea, Dan."

"Yeah! But only one girl on the ship. You can have the fish."

Tom laughed again.

"Actually," he said, "there are some women on board. Their partners smuggle them on disguised as men. I've heard that Joseph Brown on your gun is married to one of them. They reckon the captain knows all about it, but turns a blind eye."

As they talked, the ship's monkey, Captain Morgan, jumped up and pulled Tom's hair then darted off as he spun around swearing. It seemed to be fascinated with his long, blond locks. Any time it got the chance it would tug at them. Tom had thought it was funny at first, but now it was getting on his nerves. They went back to splicing rope.

Dan noticed Sam Kelly walking across to the starboard rail where he fell in with Scar's gun-crew, talking excitedly and sending up clouds of grey smoke from his clay pipe. The conversation stopped, and they all turned and looked at Dan and Tom. Abruptly, Scar nodded, then hands were spat into and shaken, Sam's small mitt all but disappearing in Scar's massive fist.

Sam strode back to the larboard side, calling Tom over.

Dan hesitated, staying where he was, but there was no ignoring Scar as he angrily motioned him over. Tight-lipped, he dragged his reluctant feet across the deck to the waiting men.

John Thatcher, a short, stocky man, well-muscled but with a belly running to flab, spoke for the gun-crew.

"We've got a wager on. Starboard side against the larboard. First one into the crow's nest wins. His watch get the other side's rum ration tonight."

Thatcher licked his flaky lips at the prospect.

A dark chill went through Dan.

"Who's our best climber?" he asked hopefully.

"It's you against your mate."

Dan's heart sank. "But I'm no good with heights. Tom's a better climber than me."

"Nonsense. Look at the size of him. He's a great, lumbering oaf. You're as agile as a monkey. You even look like one."

The rest of the men chuckled, but not Thatcher. He stuck his pock-marked face in Dan's.

"And don't let us down. We won't take kindly to losing our rum."

"But I..."

They ignored his protests and thrust him up into the rigging, his feet scrabbling on the starboard rail. Tom appeared on the larboard side and gave Dan a thumbs up.

He didn't return it.

His head span as he looked up at the swaying crow's nest, ninety feet above him. He wasn't sure he could force himself to climb more than half-way, never mind beat Tom to the masthead.

The quarterdeck stirred. The officers, sensing the excitement in the waist of the ship, crowded along the front rail, ready to enjoy the entertainment. If they knew the hands were racing for rum then there'd be a few floggings. It was against the rules to get drunk so selling or giving away your rum to another, allowing him a double ration, could get you both a taste of the cat-o-nine-tails. But sometimes they would turn a blind eye. Anything to relieve the monotony of life aboard ship.

Dan glanced over to the quarterdeck.

Oh, no!

He could see the white dress in front of the watching officers. The girl's golden hair swept around as she turned her head to look first at Tom and then at him. His chin dropped to his chest and his shoulders hunched. *Not only was he going to let down his gun-crew, he was going to embarrass himself in front of the girl.*

As Dan stood there shaking, Scar strode to the middle of the deck and raised a massive arm. Tom readied himself to spring into the sheets, but Dan just hung there, knuckles white on the ratlines, wide eyes on the dizzying masthead far above.

Scar's arm fell and a great cheer went up from the crew. Tom leapt into the rigging. Dan didn't move. John Thatcher prodded him hard with a ramrod, and he shot up. Heart in mouth, he forced himself to keep going.

The tar on the ropes covered Dan's hands and feet, making them black and slippery. But he surprised himself. He was climbing steadily, keeping up with Tom. Half-way there. As they struggled on, the cheering grew louder and Dan glanced at the deck. A mistake. Fifty feet below, the crew looked small and a long, long way down.

Dan's senses spun, dizziness taking hold of him. He shook his head, trying to clear it. He forced himself to take another step, then his feet shot out from under him, slipping off the tarred ratlines.

The jolt pulled one arm away from the ropes. Stifling a cry, he clung on with one hand, kicking with his feet, desperately trying to find a foothold as his madly beating heart threatened to shake his grip loose. The starboard watch fell silent, but the larboard side jeered and shouted for him to let go.

The wind gusted and the ship heeled over, swinging Dan back into the rigging. He grasped at the ropes like a drowning man, his scrambling feet finally finding the ratlines. He clung on, relief and fear washing over him in alternate waves.

Below him the starboard men screamed at him to climb, but he couldn't move. He could see the girl studying him with cold interest. *He couldn't let himself down in front of her. He had to climb.* He meant to reach up to the next rope but his hand remained clamped where it was, the knuckles white as it clung on with a will of its own.

The catcalls of his gun-crew had now turned to a surly silence. He imagined his dad down there watching him, felt his disapproval. *What would he think, seeing his son clinging to the rigging like a coward?*

The fingers of his right hand slowly unclenched then he forced himself to reach up and grab the next rope. His foot found the next rung and he was moving again.

A great cheer came up from below.

He was moving, but surely he must be too late?

He shot a glance over to the larboard side. To his amazement, Tom had stopped, clinging to the rigging with one hand as he swatted at Captain Morgan with the other. The monkey had taken advantage of him needing both hands to climb and was pulling his hair then jumping out of range whenever Tom let go to swipe at it.

Dan suppressed a mad urge to laugh. If he started, he

35

didn't know if he could stop again. He climbed on, desperately trying not to think of the drop.

One hand after the other. Don't think, just keep moving.

He passed Tom with only twelve feet to go. The starboard watch roared their approval and now it was the larboard side's turn to fall silent.

Tom noticed the threat and started climbing again, ignoring the monkey clinging to his head like a chattering fur hat. He shot up the rigging as if running on dry land.

Dan tried to speed up but he couldn't. All he could do was keep up the rhythm of his climb and pray.

Nearly there!

The cheering from below was almost deafening now.

Suddenly, Tom was past him. Dan watched in despair as his friend reached the lubber hole and disappeared into the crow's nest ahead of him. He felt the bile rising in his throat as his stomach tightened, threatening to spill its contents on the people below. With an effort, he forced it back down, but then the fight went out of him. He stopped climbing and just hung there. His arms and legs ached, and so did his heart.

He'd let everyone down.

Tom appeared in the crow's nest, waving to the larboard watch as they whooped and clapped. The monkey squealed in protest as Tom took a bow, but it still held on. Tom let it. He leant over and looked at Dan, hanging in the rigging beneath him.

"Hard lines mate. I thought you had me there for a minute."

It didn't make Dan feel any better. He looked at the

deck ninety feet below, and a shudder went through him. It was a long way down, and he knew what waited for him at the bottom. Scar, and an angry gun-crew.

As the larboard watch took turns slapping Tom on the back, Dan cowered in the middle of a gang of sullen men. Scar gave him a look that could have frozen the snot in an elephant's nostrils.

"I'm s-sorry, Scar. I s-said I can't climb. I d-don't like heights."

Scar growled and slammed a huge hand into his chest.

Dan shot back and cannoned into John Thatcher.

"That was deliberate," snarled the stocky man.

"It wasn't," gasped Dan. "I was pushed."

"Up there in the rigging I mean. I saw you stop to let your friend win. Had a little side-bet on it did you, the pair of you?"

John Thatcher gave him a hard shove.

"Do me out of my rum, would you?"

He pushed him again.

"I'll teach you not to cheat me."

He picked up the ramrod and advanced on Dan.

In a blur of movement, Tom charged past Dan and punched Thatcher square on the chin. He staggered, but he was a strong man and didn't go down. The crew moved back, forming a ring around them.

Thatcher held the ramrod high, circling Tom before swinging it at him with all his strength. Tom ducked and punched him in his podgy stomach. The man doubled up and Tom hit him again, knocking him to his knees. He wrenched the ramrod out of Thatcher's hands and raised it. Scar stepped forward and plucked it effortlessly from his grasp. Tom spun around, fists clenched. Scar slowly shook his head, and Tom thought better of carrying on the argument.

Commodore Cavendish had seen the whole incident from the quarterdeck. "Mr Savage? Have those men report to me for punishment."

"With pleasure, sir."

The bosun turned a mirthless smile on Tom.

"First week at sea and yer gonna be introduced to the Captain's Daughter already."

"I thought she was his niece," said Tom.

The bosun gave an evil chuckle. "The 'Captain's Daughter' is the cat, Bailey. The cat-o-nine-tails. A few lashes of that and ye'll have no skin left on yer back worth talking about. I've seen stronger men than you, die under her tender kiss."

John Thatcher lay doubled up, blood oozing from a cut lip. The bosun turned to Scar.

"Get him cleaned up then bring the pair of 'em to the captain's cabin."

Philip Cavendish glared at John Thatcher and Tom. "I'll not have fighting on my ship. Not until we get at the Spaniards anyway. You can fight to your heart's content then, but not before."

He rose from his desk and walked to the stern window, staring out over the ocean for a few minutes before turning back to the room.

"John Thatcher, you should know better. You're an able seaman. I expect you to act as an example to the ship's boys, not brawl with them. I could disrate you but you're too good a sailor to be demoted down amongst the lubbers in the waist of the ship. I'll not have you as a waister. You'll receive half a dozen lashes instead."

John Thatcher's head dropped and he looked glumly at his feet.

"Tom Bailey."

Tom straightened his back.

"I realise that you are not used to the ways of the Royal Navy, and that you were trying to help a friend. In view of your age and inexperience I am minded to be lenient with you on this occasion. You will have your rum ration stopped for a week and you will attend closely to John Thatcher's flogging so that you know what to expect if you break the rules in the future."

"That's not fair," Thatcher blurted out. "He was–"

The bosun's rope came down on his back, cutting his complaint short.

"Make that a dozen lashes, Mr Savage," said the captain softly. "And make sure they are laid on well."

He turned back to the scowling sailor.

"Anything else you'd like to say, Thatcher?"

"No, sir."

"Good. Punishment not to be carried out until six bells tomorrow morning."

The captain paused and treated Tom to a brief smile.

"I wouldn't want to stop Master Bailey from celebrating his victory tonight. From what I saw, I think he has the makings of a good topman. That will be all thank you gentlemen."

Thatcher glared his hatred at Tom as they were led out.

At supper that evening, mugs of rum surreptitiously changed hands as the starboard watch reluctantly passed over their ration to the grinning larbowlines. Tom happily drank away his double share and even had his mug topped up by his admiring messmates. He'd won the race, secured the rum, and thrashed one of Scar's feared gun-crew. That night, he could do no wrong. Meanwhile, Dan picked at his food in silence, being pointedly ignored by Scar, Thatcher, and the rest of his surly table.

When the drums sounded on deck, beating the men to quarters, as they did every evening after supper, the larboard watch got to their battle stations considerably later than the starbowlines. The captain called an unwelcome gunnery practise for the upper gun-deck, and all thirteen of the starboard cannons had fired in quick succession before a ragged tattoo started on the larboard side. Commodore Cavendish watched with suspicion, but said nothing. Sometimes the men had to be left to their fun. They'd be surly enough in the morning. None of them liked to see a flogging.

No one was unhappy when the end of the second dog-watch sounded and all hammocks were piped down. They were pleased at the chance to get some sleep. The larboard hands were boisterous at first, but soon dozed off into drunken stupors.

As the men slept a dark shape detached itself from the shadows and flitted through the hammocks, moving stealthily towards Dan. It froze as he stirred, then slunk back into the gloom.

Dan gave a shudder as he lay awake listening to the snores, farts and coughs that filled the fo'c'sle. Tom seemed to be taking to life at sea far better than he was, but that didn't surprise him. Tom took everything in his stride. He envied him his easy self-confidence and ability to get on with people. Dan wasn't like that, but he would get through this. *He had to. He was here to find his dad.* He took out his silver locket and clutched it to his chest.

Greedy eyes watched from the shadows. After a few moments the dark shape slid noiselessly away, pausing briefly by a swinging hammock before disappearing into the gloom.

Dan decided he would talk to the captain in the morning. He would ask him about his dad. The thought made him feel a little better, and he finally gave in to exhaustion and fell into a deep and dreamless sleep.

CHAPTER 5

A QUARREL

A shrill whistle snapped Dan awake. The dark room swung dizzily as he tried to focus his eyes and his brain. All around him muted voices mumbled oaths and curses.

"All hands, ahoy!"

Dan recognised the bosun's booming voice and slid out of his hammock, wiping the night's sleep from his bleary eyes.

"Up all hammocks!"

Men rushed to untie and roll their bedding, ready to stow it on deck. Some hammocks still swayed in the semi-darkness and Dan could see Tom's shock of blond hair sticking up in one of them. The bosun stood beside it, a wicked-looking blade in his hand.

"A sharp knife, a clear conscience, and out or down is the word," he cried.

Tom didn't stir.

The bosun's knife came up in one fast movement, and cut the lanyard at the top of the hammock. Tom tumbled to the floor.

He jumped up holding his head. "Who did that? I'll kill him!"

The blade flashed in the bosun's hand and stopped at Tom's throat. "Ye'll not be killing anyone, boy. Now roll that hammock and get yerself on deck. Move!"

Tom stood his ground for a second then, to Dan's relief, said, "Good morning to you too, Bosun. It's handy to have you around now that my ma's not here to wake me."

With that he rolled his bedding and headed for the hatch.

Meanwhile, the bosun's mates were handing out similar treatment to other tardy members of the crew, all of them larbowlines — men of the larboard watch. Loud thumps and curses could be heard throughout the fo'c'sle. Dan skirted past the bosun who was beating Henry Hall with his knotted rope as the boy cowered in his hammock. Without a backwards glance, he followed Tom out of the hatchway.

After they had stowed away their bedding, a bosun's mate handed them brooms and told them to clean the deck before it was holystoned. They soon discovered this was an unpleasant task as the ship's animals had been allowed to roam the previous evening, and they'd all left souvenirs for the boys to clear up. Tom turned green as he regarded the steaming piles, and he cursed last night's rum.

In the chill of the morning, Dan pulled his jacket closely around him, glad of the new clothes. The breeze stiffened and the ship began to pitch and roll. He swayed in time with the heaving deck, and a smile touched his mouth as he watched Tom stumbling around in his ill-fitting outfit. Tom had yet to find his sea legs and moved like a baby foal on ice.

"That was a nice dive you did this morning," Dan laughed as he swept the deck. "Very stylish. But the old hands tell me it's safer to get down feet first?"

"You'll be going somewhere feet first if you don't watch it," growled Tom.

Dan leant on his broom and looked at his friend. "Do you know what day it is, Tom? It's the eighteenth of November 1719."

"So what?"

Tom wrinkled his nose and dry heaved as he picked up a wet turd left by Captain Morgan. He tossed it overboard, wiping his hands on his new trousers.

"I'm starting to hate that bloody monkey!" he coughed.

"It's our fifteenth birthday," said Dan.

"Oh yeah!"

Tom brightened up, holding out a mucky hand.

"Happy birthday, mate."

Dan looked warily at the outstretched hand, and thought better of shaking it. Instead he held out his broom.

"Happy birthday, Tom. It's not much but..."

"This is embarrassing. I've got you the same thing."

Tom passed *his* broom to Dan.

"You two," yelled the bosun. "What do ye think yer playing at? Get back to work!"

They grinned at each other but quickly obeyed.

When they'd finished they joined the men holystoning the deck. They had to pull heavy, polished stones back and forth across the watered and sanded timbers until they were smooth and bright. It was boring, back-breaking work and the effect didn't last long. When they asked what the point was, Sam told them it was just to keep idle hands busy and warned them they'd be doing this every morning for the rest of the voyage. But at least it gave them a chance to be together.

Dan whistled with relief when breakfast was called.

"About time," he said, "I'm gutfoundered. I could eat a scabby dog."

"I could eat a scabby monkey," growled Tom, scraping the muck from his hands as well as he could. "And I swear I will, if I ever catch the bloody thing."

Dan ate at Tom's table, ignoring the bosun's warning. One glance at his own messmates, and he decided to keep well out of their way. All of them cast sullen looks in his direction, but John Thatcher glared pure hatred.

"What?" snapped Dan when he couldn't stand it any longer. "I lost a stupid race. So what!"

"I was robbed last night," snarled Thatcher. "You wouldn't know anything about that would you, Leake? Skulking over there out of the way. You wouldn't happen to have a new pocket knife, would you?"

"I'm not a thief," sputtered Dan, reddening. "Why are you blaming me?"

"You don't rob aboard a ship. Every sailor knows that. But you and your mate ain't sailors, are you?. Only a landlubber would even think of it. And Bailey was too fuddled with drink to think at all. That leaves you!"

Tom jumped up. "Leave him alone, Puff-guts, or I'll give you another beating!"

45

"It will be with knives next time, Sonny," growled Thatcher, rising to his feet.

"Anytime you want!"

A bosun's mate grabbed Tom by the shoulder.

"Sit down, Bailey. You're in enough trouble already. Don't make it worse for yourself."

Tom fumed for a second and then flung himself back down, dismembering his meal with his workknife. Watching his friend's vicious attack on his food, Dan almost felt sorry for John Thatcher, who continued to scowl at them from the other table.

"You want to pick your enemies more carefully, lads," said Sam Kelly. "Thatcher may not look much but if you ever saw him with a cutlass in his hand and a Spaniard in front of him, you'd think twice before you crossed him."

"He doesn't worry me," grunted Tom, ramming his food into his mouth.

"And as for Scar? He isn't even human. I've seen a boarding party cut down to a man by grapeshot, but nothing touched him. He went over the rail on his own and it must have been five minutes before we could get anyone across to help him. There was Scar, standing amongst a pile of Spanish bodies, not a mark on him. The Spaniards were trampling each other trying to get away from him. I tell you, he's a fiend from hell not a human being. Keep well away from him."

"I can't, can I?" groaned Dan, pushing his unfinished plate from him, his eyes flicking over to Scar.

The giant glowered back, along with the rest of his murderous-looking messmates.

"Let's get up on deck, Tom. I'm not popular down here and I don't want the bosun catching me at this table again."

Tom quickly polished off what was left of Dan's breakfast, then they made their way topside and stalked towards the quarterdeck. The girl appeared, as if she'd been waiting for them.

"Hello," she said sweetly, her big eyes on Tom. "My name's Emily."

"I'm Dan."

She didn't even turn her head towards him.

"I'm Tom."

"Pleased to meet you, Tom," she purred, holding out a small, delicate hand.

"Emily!"

They all jumped, then Dan and Tom quickly touched a forelock in salute when they saw Commodore Cavendish glaring down from the quarterdeck.

"Leave the boys alone and get back to your cabin."

She flashed Tom a brilliant smile before gliding through the doorway and out of sight.

Dan glanced over at his friend. The big, silly grin on his stupid face, set his teeth on edge. Fists clenching of their own accord, he stepped towards him, his mouth tightening into a thin slit.

"I can't believe you're trying to steal my girl."

"She's not your girl."

"Oh! So you *are* trying to steal her then?"

"No!" Tom thought for a second. "She's just not yours, that's all."

Dan turned and stomped off to the bows, wanting to be

as far away from Tom as he could get in the close, wooden world of a ship. He sat brooding on the bowsprit until the call for gunnery practise snapped him from his angry thoughts.

As he skidded to a halt in front of his gun, Scar cuffed him on the side of the head. Dan staggered and looked around in pain and confusion.

"Powder!" yelled Thatcher.

Of course!

Dan grabbed a container and scurried to the hatchway, making his way down to the magazine in the depths of the ship, well below the water line to protect it from hot cannonballs. He noticed Tom duck into the room ahead of him. As he hurried down into the darkness he could just make out Tom's outline. In silence, he quickly sealed his container before springing back to his feet.

Tom knelt in front of him, scrabbling for a cartridge in the dark. With his blood still boiling, Dan plucked up his courage, took aim, and then kicked him up the arse with all his might.

"What the…"

Dan was halfway up the stairs and running like he'd never run before.

"Who the hell was that? You're gonna die!"

As he ran, Dan could hear footsteps raging up the staircase behind him, but he had a good head start. He managed to clear each flight before Tom could catch sight of his attacker. He hurled himself through the hatchway, shot across the deck and was safely back at his gun before Tom's furious head appeared at the hatch, twisting around like an owl's, trying to see where the culprit had gone.

Captain Morgan spotted him and scampered over to pull his hair. He took one look at Tom's contorted face and ran off to tease the ship's dog instead. Tom stomped off to his gun, muttering to himself and rubbing his bum.

Dan let out a sigh of relief. *He'd got away with it.* He turned to the cannon and bumped straight into Scar. He flicked a worried glance up at the giant but, to his amazement, Scar's shaven head nodded in what seemed to be approval. The rest of the gun-crew looked impressed as well, apart from John Thatcher who maintained his customary scowl.

The cannon loader, Joseph Brown, patted Dan on the shoulder.

"Keep that up and you'll do okay," he said grudgingly. "You're the fastest powder monkey we've ever had."

CHAPTER 6

CAT-O-NINE-TAILS

The next day passed slowly as Dan fell into the monotonous rhythm of the ship's routine. He worked automatically, his mind elsewhere as he methodically scrubbed the deck. A sudden shout from the crow's nest snapped him out of his daydream.

"Ship ahoy!" called the lookout.

The whole place came to life, buzzing with excitement. Dan spun around and scanned the immense ocean, but could see nothing.

"Where away?" cried the officer of the watch.

"Off the larboard bow. Hull down on the horizon."

"Inform the captain please, Mister Savage," called young Lieutenant Trimble, hurrying to the weather rail and jerkily raising his spyglass.

Dan ran to the side and peered at the horizon. He could see nothing but sea and sky.

Tom shuffled up, tenderly rubbing his bum. "I can't see a thing mate, how about you?"

"Nothing!" he snapped, still angry.

Tom knew how he felt about, Emily. 'Emily'. At least

he knew her name now. Fat lot of use that was going to do him!

Tom refused to take the hint. "Fancy going up in the rigging for a better look?"

"Go up yourself!" Dan forced the words out through gritted teeth.

"Okay." Tom swung himself easily into the rigging and scrambled up.

Commodore Cavendish appeared on the quarterdeck. "Can you see her colours, Lookout?"

"No, sir."

"Keep your eyes peeled. Shout out when you do."

"Aye Aye, sir."

The captain called the bosun over. "Topmen aloft if you please, Mister Savage."

"Topmen aloft," bellowed the bosun.

The rigging came alive with men climbing and scurrying in all directions.

"Helmsman. Come about and bear towards that ship."

The other vessel could now be plainly seen. It carried full sail and was heading straight for them.

As the *Dover* turned onto its new bearing, the topmen darted through the rigging, trimming the sails. The gap between the two ships closed rapidly now that they were on a convergent course.

The captain peered through his spyglass. "Let's not take any chances. Beat to quarters."

"Beat to quarters," yelled the bosun.

The drums started up and men and boys flew to their action stations. Shouts of command and the whistles of bosun's mates pierced the air. Dan ran to his gun as fast as he could. He saw Scar glowering at him and veered off to the hatchway, heading for the magazine. Other powder monkeys scampered up and down the steps, cartridge cases in their hands.

Dan plunged into the darkened room, knowing his way by instinct now. His heart pounded in his ribcage. *This time it was for real.* He scrabbled amongst the cartridges, shoving one into his canister and slamming the lid on tight. Sam Kelly had warned him what would happen if a spark landed in an open container. He raced back the way he'd come and threw himself out of the hatchway and onto the deck. He reached the gun and held out the cartridge to John Thatcher, who grabbed it and rammed it down the barrel of the cannon. Dan dashed off again.

As he got back, gasping for breath, he saw Joseph Brown pushing a round shot into the muzzle, followed by a cloth wad to stop it from rolling out again. Then John Thatcher rammed them both down. The gun-crew grabbed the ropes either side of the heavy cannon and ran it out of the open gun-port, ready for firing.

Over the rail, he could see the sails of the enemy ship growing rapidly closer. He held out the next cartridge.

"Put that away, you fool," yelled Thatcher, brandishing the ramrod. "Do you want to blow us all up? One charge at a time."

Dan hastily shoved the cartridge back into the container and sealed it, glancing fearfully at the nearing warship.

"White Ensign showing," called the lookout.

"Stand the men down," ordered the captain. "She's one

of ours."

Dan stood sweating by the cannon, a mixture of relief and disappointment washing over him. There was to be no battle after all. His heart still thumped heavily in his chest as he moved to the rail and watched the other ship drawing ever closer. As the rhythm of the *Dover* slowly returned to normal, so did Dan's breathing, and he let out a deep sigh.

"Shall I call the men up to witness punishment, Cap'n? It's nearly six bells." The bosun couldn't keep the eagerness from his voice.

"Not now," said the captain irritably. "I've more important matters to attend to. And I know what time it is, Mister Savage."

"Yes, sir."

Commodore Cavendish regarded the bosun's retreating back. The man was good at his job, but why did he have to be so damned keen to see the blood of his own shipmates? There'd be plenty to go around soon enough if his instincts were right. He turned back to the rail as the frigate hove-to and lowered its boat.

Sailors ran to hang a ladder over the side as the launch reached the *Dover*.

"Captain Lawrence, *Aldborough*. Permission to come on board, sir?"

"Permission granted."

The crew looked on with interest. If the *Aldborough's* captain himself was coming on board, then it must be important news. As he stepped aboard, the bosun's mates lined-up and blew their whistles in salute. The two captains retreated to the grand cabin, already deep in heated debate.

An excited buzz spread through the ship as the seamen guessed at what was being discussed.

"We'll be in action before the day is out," claimed an old hand.

Dan felt his blood race. *What would a sea-battle be like?* He pictured himself firing the cannon then boarding the Spaniard, cutlass in hand. *Or would he run? Would he turn out to be a coward?* This scared him far more than the thought of facing the enemy.

Twenty minutes later, Captain Lawrence returned to the *Aldborough*. The fast frigate quickly got under way, heading south. On the *Dover*, Commodore Cavendish strode onto the quarterdeck and called for all hands to be assembled. Once again excitement buzzed around the ship as the men waited to hear the news.

The bosun drew himself up to his full height, smirking at the expectant faces below him.

"All hands, prepare to witness punishment," he called.

A stunned silence greeted his words. In their excitement the men had forgotten about the flogging. A low, angry, rumble began to steadily rise.

"Quiet!" yelled the bosun.

The noise died down to sullen murmurs as red-coated marines lined the quarterdeck, muskets in hand.

The master-at-arms and a marine flanked John Thatcher as they marched him up on deck. Two bosun's mates seized him, stripped the shirt from his back, and lashed him upright to a wooden grating. They then stood either side of the unfortunate man. They always had two men on hand at a flogging so that, when one tired, the other could take over and keep up the strength of the blows as the punishment went on.

One of the men pulled the cat-o-nine-tails out from the red cloth bag that protected it from drying out in the salt air. It had to be kept supple to inflict maximum pain. The bosun walked up and took the cat from the man, sending him away. He liked to attend to a flogging in person.

"They've let the cat out of the bag," muttered Sam Kelly. "He's for it now."

Another marine forced Tom over to stand facing Thatcher, only a few feet from him. He looked even more miserable than the man about to be whipped.

Lieutenant Trimble was on flogging duty.

"All r-ready, Captain," he called in a small voice.

"Carry on, Mr Trimble. A dozen lashes, if you please."

The young officer gave an involuntary shudder, then stepped back. "L-Lay on, M-Mr Savage."

The bosun slowly shook out the cat-o-nine-tails to its full length. Dan stared at the instrument of torture with horrified fascination. Attached to a two-foot-long pole were nine knotted cords of the same length, each about a quarter of an inch thick. The bosun carefully untangled it before pulling the cat back over his shoulder. He waited a few seconds, enjoying the tension, then brought the lash down, whipping it into the man's bare back with all his strength.

Thatcher's whole body convulsed, the breath hissing from his mouth, but he didn't cry out. Nine long, red welts rose up on his white, naked flesh.

Dan noticed Emily on the quarterdeck. She stared avidly at the sickening scene, her mouth half open. As Dan watched, her tongue flicked out and she wet her lips.

"One!" cried Lieutenant Trimble.

The bosun brought his brawny arm up again, and leant into the next blow as he brutally hammered the whip across the sailor's shoulders. Beside him, Tom recoiled as bits of flesh jumped into his face. This time a low moan escaped Thatcher's lips and blood began to trickle down his back. The low, angry rumble of the crew started up once more.

Dan looked up at Emily. Her bright green eyes were fixed on the poor man's back, and her full lips had curled up into a smile.

"T-two!" called Lieutenant Trimble.

The cat-o-nine-tails, blood dripping from its ends, came slowly back over the bosun's right shoulder as he prepared for the next blow. On the quarterdeck, Emily licked her lips again.

"Forebear!" cried the captain.

After a moment of disbelief, the crew roared their approval.

"But that was only two, sir," cried the bosun, disappointment etched in every word.

"I can count thank you, Mr Savage," snapped Commodore Cavendish. "I've had some news, and we're going to need every man fighting fit by the end of the week. Now cut him down."

Dan looked up. The smile had vanished from Emily's face, replaced by a petulant scowl.

John Thatcher finally let out a cry when the bosun tossed a bucket of salt water onto his bloody, battered back. His shirt was thrown over his shoulders and the bosun's mates cut him down from the grating.

Philip Cavendish stood patiently while Thatcher made his way, slowly but unaided, to where his messmates waited. The captain was pleased with himself. Punishment had been carried out but he had still managed to get the men on his side. A sullen, resentful crew would be no good in battle.

Finally he spoke. "Men, we're in for a fight!"

A loud cheer echoed around the ship.

"And tonight there'll be a double ration of rum!"

The men shouted themselves hoarse.

CHAPTER 7

ADMIRAL LEAKE

Musket balls cracked across the bow, marines firing at a target they'd hung from the fore yardarm. Dan ducked away and headed aft. As he weaved along the busy deck, dodging milling sailors practising with cutlasses, his eyes searched the ship. He found Tom sitting near the quarterdeck, mending his damaged hammock.

"Tom, I..."

"Oh! You're talking to me now, are you?"

"I'm sorry, Tom. I've been acting like an idiot."

"You don't need to act like an idiot, you are one!"

After a long moment, Tom's scowling face relaxed and he smiled.

"Sit down and give me a hand with this bloody hammock. Savage is a proper pig, isn't he?"

"That's something we *can* agree on," laughed Dan, as he joined his friend and began to splice together two ends of cut rope.

Tom shifted in discomfort, and gently rubbed his backside.

"Yesterday in the powder magazine, some little shit

kicked me up the arse. I've got a massive bruise."

"Really?" said Dan, looking away and drumming his fingers on the deck. "I wonder who that could have been."

"I'll bet it was that little runt, Henry Hall. It's the sort of sneaky thing you'd expect from him. He wouldn't stand up to someone face to face, like you or I would."

"No," said Dan, feeling the colour flooding into his cheeks.

He coughed nervously.

"But it might not have been him."

"Who else would pull a dirty, rotten trick like that?"

"Um... Actually..."

Dan took a long, deep breath.

"I've no idea!"

"Mark my words," fumed Tom. "It will have been him, sneaky little runt that he is!"

Dan decided that a change of subject might be in order.

"Have you heard what's happening?"

His friend always seemed to know what was going on.

Tom's head turned this way and that as he checked around him.

"We're meeting up with the *Norwich* and the *Advice*."

He lowered his voice as he spotted Scar at a nearby cannon, using a wet rag to clean out the touch hole.

"The word is that three Spanish war-ships have sneaked out of Santander and are heading for Cadiz. We're to cut them off. They reckon we'll catch up with them by the end of the week."

Dan noticed the quiver of excitement in his friend's voice.

"You're looking forward to it, are you?"

Tom's head came up, his eyebrows knitted as he studied Dan's face.

"Course I am. Aren't you?"

"Um… Yeah! Can't wait to get at 'em."

Tom grinned and punched him lightly on the arm.

"Don't worry Dan, it'll be a piece of cake. You'll have the luck of the Irish with you."

Behind them, Scar pricked up his ears and stared intently at Dan before moving away, deep in thought.

With the enemy nowhere to be seen, time seemed to crawl by as they ploughed doggedly on through the Atlantic swell. Despite the prospect of a battle in the near future, they still scrubbed and holystoned the deck for hours every morning before eating. After breakfast it was gunnery drill until noon, when dinner and a welcome tot of rum broke up the long day. An evening training session had been added to the routine one in the morning but, to save ammunition, they now practised without powder and shot, merely going through the motions – a long, tiresome, pointless-seeming pantomime, played out twice a day.

One dark overcast morning, Henry Hall slunk past the starboard cannons on his way to gunnery practise. He paused as he came level with Dan.

"Thief," he hissed out of the corner of his mouth.

Dan spun around, not sure that he'd heard right, but the bosun whacked the pimple-faced powder monkey across the back with the end of his knotted rope, sending him scampering away to his cannon. The burly man followed him across the deck, lashing at the skinny boy as he tried to crawl beneath the barrel of the gun.

"Always loitering, aren't ye?" bellowed the bosun as he brought the thick rope down again. "This may seem like a game to ye now, but we'll be playing for keeps soon enough! Now get yerself down to the magazine. Move!"

Savage swung the knotted rope one last time as Henry Hall ran, squealing, past him.

Dan watched the scrawny powder monkey scurry away, then frowned when he remembered what he'd said. But as the rest of the morning dragged by in the tiresome, repetitive gunnery drill, he put the incident out of his mind and sunk into a trance-like routine.

When they were at last piped down for dinner, Dan once again shunned his own gun-crew and joined Tom and his messmates at their table. He frowned when his greetings went unanswered as he sat down.

He tried again.

"I'll be happy when these ruddy gunnery drills fin..."

Dan trailed off, his words greeted with silence. No one looked up and he fidgeted with his bowl as he squinted at the host of down-turned heads. Everyone pointedly ignored him.

"What's going on?" he hissed at Tom.

"That runt Henry Hall has been putting it around that you're a thief," whispered Tom. "Says he was robbed in his sleep last night, but woke up and saw you sneaking back to your hammock."

Dan sat open-mouthed.

"He's lying. He's a liar."

"I know that," said Tom, "but someone's thieving, and Hall's pointed the finger at you. Most of the men are just taking his word for it. It's all over the larboard watch. The whole ship will know by supper!"

Dan's head snapped up.

"Know what? I haven't done anything!"

"Of course you haven't."

Tom laid a restraining hand on Dan's arm as he tried to rise from the table.

"But they all believe the lying little sneak. You'll have to watch your back until this is sorted."

"I'll sort him tonight," snarled Dan. "After hammocks are piped down. I'll make him pay for this."

"And how's that going to look?" said Tom. "You sneaking about the fo'c'sle after lights out. They'll think you're the thief for sure."

Tom threw a quick glance around the mess deck.

"And keep your voice down. We don't want everyone knowing our business."

"Then what can I do?" whispered Dan at the top of his voice. "I can't just let the lying rat get away with it. What would you do, if you were me?"

"I'd beat the living tar out of him."

"Well then!"

"But I'm not you," said Tom. "You should use your brains. That's what you're good at. Keep your head down for now. The real thief will slip up sooner or later."

That night, tired out with the extra training, the men soon drifted off into a deep sleep. As Dan dozed, a shadowy figure crept through the fo'c'sle then crouched beneath his hammock, listening carefully. Satisfied by his gentle snoring, a hand reached up into Dan's jacket pocket. It emerged clutching the silver locket. The figure silently disappeared back into the darkness.

The boys were busy 'working up junk' – unpicking old lengths of tarred rope. The resulting 'oakum', would be used to caulk leaky timbers. They laboured in silence, each deep in his own thoughts.

Dan absent-mindedly reached inside his shirt, then suddenly jumped up.

"My locket!"

He frantically patted his pockets, then turned them inside out.

"It's gone!"

"You must have dropped it, mate."

They retraced their footsteps to the fo'c'sle, but found nothing. A bosun's mate chased them out with a rope-end, ordering them back to work.

They returned to their job but Dan was frantic.

"It's been stolen. I know it. I'll report it to the captain."

"You don't snitch to officers, Dan. The men will think you worse than a thief. We have to sort this ourselves. Have you any idea who it could have been?"

Dan's face darkened.

"I've got my suspicions."

"It won't be Thatcher," mused Tom. "I know he said that you robbed him, but this isn't how he'd retaliate. Slitting your throat would be more his style."

"No, not him."

"Then who?"

"Like you said, I have to sort this out myself."

"I said, 'ourselves'. You know I've got your back."

"No!"

Dan's voice was a feral snarl.

"I'll sort it myself. This is personal."

Tom shrugged.

"Well, you know where I am if you need me, mate."

They returned to picking oakum.

As he worked, Dan thought of his father. The loss of the locket concentrated his mind and he came to a decision he knew he should have made a long time ago.

"I'm going to see the captain," he told Tom.

"We've been through that already, haven't we? You don't snitch to officers."

"That's not why I want to see him, Tom. I'm going to ask him about my dad."

Tom pursed his lips.

"It's not the best time, Dan. We're heading into battle. The captain will have other things on his mind."

Dan shook his head.

"I can't wait any longer. I'll burst. I need to know about my dad."

Tom knew that he'd not be able to talk him out of it. Once Dan made his mind up about something, he stuck to it like a barnacle to a ship's hull.

"You can't just go up to the captain, Dan. You need to talk to Scar first. Well, maybe not him. You'll have to speak to the bosun."

"I can't talk to him! He hates me!"

"He hates everyone. If you want to see the captain, what choice do you have? You'll be flogged if you speak to an officer without being spoken to first."

A rustle of clothing interrupted their conversation, and Emily stood before them.

"Hello, Tom," she purred, ignoring Dan as usual.

Dan carried on splicing the rope. He didn't look up.

"Hi Emily," said Tom, smiling up at her and trying to catch her eye.

But for once she was looking at Dan.

"Cat got your tongue?" she asked petulantly.

Dan stiffened. *Yes, the cat did have his tongue — the cat-o-nine-tails. He remembered the look on her face during the flogging.* He ignored her and continued working on the split rope.

Emily pouted. "A gentleman would stand up when a lady addresses him."

"Well I'm not a gentleman," snapped Dan.

He looked her up and down.

"And you're not a lady!"

She gave a small gasp as if she'd been slapped. The angelic mask slipped for a moment, her eyes narrowing to angry slits.

"You can't talk to me like that!"

"I don't want to talk to you at all."

Dan turned his back and returned to his work.

Eyes blazing, she grabbed Tom by the arm.

"Are you going to let him talk to me like that?"

"Apologise to her right now," Tom barked.

Dan carried on working.

Emily glared at him for a moment longer, and then stamped her foot and stormed off in an angry swirl of petticoats.

Tom turned on him.

"What's wrong with you?"

"Nothing!" snapped Dan as he finished splicing the frayed rope and threw it down.

He got up.

Forget Tom. Forget Emily. You're here to find your dad, so you need to talk to the bosun.

His legs shook slightly as he walked over, partly from anger and partly from fear.

"What do ye want, Leake?"

The bosun's face wore its usual, unfriendly scowl.

Dan pressed on anyway.

"I want to see the captain, Mister Savage."

"Oh! Ye do, do ye? Well I doubt if the cap'n wants to see you."

"It's about my dad."

The bosun's face broke into an unpleasant grin.

"Orphans aren't allowed to have dads, Leake. It's the first rule of being an orphan."

Dan said nothing.

"What about yer dad?"

"He's in the navy."

Dan thought about it. He'd been serving for nine years so, knowing his father, he'd have been promoted by now. He nodded to himself.

"He's an officer."

"Officer, my hairy backside!" snapped the bosun, then he stopped and looked hard at Dan, the poorly-oiled cogs of his brain grinding slowly away.

Stranger things happened at sea. Young lads stowed away for all sorts of reasons. The boy certainly wasn't typical of the gutter sweepings that usually ended up on a British man-o-war. And the name 'Leake' rang a bell somewhere. He came to a decision.

"Come with me young sir, if ye please? The cap'n might want to see ye after all."

The bosun led Dan up to the quarterdeck and waited to be acknowledged. After some time, the captain nodded to him.

"Wait here please, Master Leake," said the bosun.

He marched across to the weather side of the deck and, after a brief conversation with Commodore Cavendish, waved Dan over to join them.

The captain nonchalantly returned Dan's smart salute.

"Mister Savage tells me that your father is a naval officer. Is that correct?"

"Yes, sir."

"I knew you were hiding something when you signed on. You can read and write, can't you? Do you think I'm stupid?"

"Yes, sir."

The captain fixed him with an icy glare.

Dan gulped.

"I mean no, sir."

He hurried on before he could lose his nerve.

"But yes, I can read and write."

"I thought so."

Commodore Cavendish smiled.

"I've heard of most of the officers on the Navy List. The only 'Leake' I know is Admiral Leake. He wouldn't be your father by any chance now, would he?"

Dan's mouth fell open.

"Admiral Leake?"

He meant it as a question, but the captain took it as an answer and put a paternal hand on Dan's shoulder.

"Why did you stow away rather than sign on as a midshipman? I presume it was your father's idea to toughen you up. That would be just like him. You see I know your father. Sir John Leake. A fine man."

Dan frowned.

"No, sir. Daniel Leake. My father's Daniel Leake."

"Daniel Leake?"

"He was pressed back in–"

"Pressed? A Pressed man?"

The captain's voice rose to a shout.

"Mister Savage. Get this fool off my quarterdeck!"

The bosun grabbed Dan by the collar, dragged him to the stairway and flung him down. As he lay in a pile at the foot of the steps, the bosun arrived and kicked him hard in the ribs. Dan struggled painfully to his feet and retreated across the deck as the big man rained blows on him with his knotted rope.

"I'll teach ye to make a fool of me in front of the cap'n," he yelled, raising his arm for another strike.

The blow didn't fall. Scar was suddenly there, standing between Dan and the furious bosun.

"Get out of my way, Scar!"

The giant didn't move.

"I'm warning ye. Get out of my way or ye'll feel the end of my rope."

A low growl came from deep in Scar's throat.

Savage took a step back, his eyes darting left and right, looking for the bosun's mates. No help arrived.

Scar lumbered towards him.

"It's death to strike a ship's officer," squawked the bosun, ducking down.

The rest of the gun-crew pressed around.

"Don't do it Scar. He's not worth it."

The bosun took another step back then, realising that Scar wasn't coming after him, he straightened up.

"Get back to yer work!" he shouted, lashing out at the nearest man as he stalked away.

Tom found Dan huddled in a corner of the fo'c'sle, his knees drawn up to his chin and his arms wrapped around them. He rocked slowly backwards and forwards, his eyes tight shut. Tom looked down at his friend, forgetting their recent quarrel. He seemed to have shrunk to half his normal size.

"Did he hurt you bad?"

Dan's red-rimmed eyes turned to Tom.

"It's not that. It's my dad. I really thought that I was going to find him, but now…?"

"We'll still find him, mate."

Dan shook his head and wiped the back of his hand across his nose.

"We're stuck on this stinking ship, without a clue where he is. I don't even have his portrait now. It was a stupid idea. I shouldn't have dragged you into this."

"To be honest, I kind of like it here," said Tom. "And we *will* find your dad. I know we will."

Dan said nothing for a couple of minutes, then eventually looked up, blinking back tears.

"Thanks, Tom," he whispered.

"No problem, mate."

Tom settled himself down beside his friend, and they sat in silence with no need for words.

CHAPTER 8

THE STORM

The next few days were a misery for Dan. Crewmen from the larboard watch hissed, 'thief', every time they passed him. They ignored his pleas that he had been robbed as well. The only consolation was that, to his amazement, his messmates stood by him. Anyone threatening violence against him was quickly made aware that they'd be taking on the whole of Scar's gun-crew. They soon backed off, but the sneers continued.

Dan found himself eating with his own messmates again. John Thatcher still scowled at him and Scar remained silent, but the others seemed friendly enough.

"I appreciate you standing up for me," said Dan. "But I don't understand. I thought you all hated me?"

"If we hate you that's our business, nobody else's," growled Thatcher.

Joseph Brown took a friendlier tone. "What he means is we stick up for our messmates. That's how it is in the navy. Don't get me wrong, if we find proof that you've stolen from us then we'll tip you overboard one dark night, but we'll not let anyone else touch one of our own. It's messmate before a shipmate; shipmate before a stranger; and stranger before a dog. Remember that next time you're thinking of eating at another table."

"But you don't think I'm the thief, do you?"

John Thatcher looked hard at him. "So you've never stolen anything in your life then?"

Dan hesitated. "I stole food sometimes after my mum died. I had to. I'd no money. I had to eat."

The stocky sailor withered him with a scornful glare, but Joseph Brown intervened again.

"We don't think you're the thief, Dan. We know your locket was stolen, and we know you don't have John Thatcher's pocket knife."

"But how?"

"We checked your pockets while you were asleep," grunted Thatcher.

"And your mate's pockets as well," said Joseph Brown. "Nothing! You're both as poor as church mice."

Dan felt a brief flush of anger, but went to bed that night feeling slightly better than before.

The black squall came out of nowhere, tossing the ship around like a cork in a storm drain.

"All hands on deck!" cried the bosun, his call hardly audible over the screaming wind and crashing waves.

Dan and the others, jolted out of their sleep by the violent tossing of the ship, were already making their way up the companionway, knowing they would be needed topside. A great wave broke over the bows and washed down the open hatch, drenching them before they'd even reached the pitching deck. The skies were black and the surging sea as dark as the night itself, the moon and stars hidden behind banks of rain-sodden clouds.

"You two," shouted the bosun as Dan and Tom emerged, soaking, from the hatchway. "Get up in the rigging. Help get the mainsail down."

Dan shuddered as he looked up at the violently swaying mast. "B-but I'm not a topman!"

"Move!" yelled the bosun. "If that sail ain't down fast the mast will be carried overboard. Then ye'll drown along with the rest of us."

"Come on!" Tom, pulled on Dan's arm. "Stick with me. It'll be a piece of cake."

He half-dragged Dan to the rigging and pushed him up in front of him.

"Start climbing," he shouted. "I'll be right behind you."

Dan gritted his teeth and started up the ropes. Spray lashed into him as he climbed, the howling wind sucking the breath from his lungs.

As the ship pitched heavily, a vision of falling flashed through his mind. He was spinning over and over, plunging down towards the heaving ocean, his mouth open in a silent scream.

"Keep going!" yelled Tom, snapping him back to reality. "Keep moving!"

Dan willed himself on and crawled up the sodden rigging to the top of the mainsail then edged out along the yard arm with Tom shouting encouragement as he followed him out on the swinging foot rope. The ship bucked and heeled with every blast of wind or surge of the sea. Dan hung on with one hand, knuckles white, as he frantically helped to furl the sail with his other.

Tom whooped with delight as the ship heeled right over, the mast almost level with the broiling sea. The wild sound mingled with Dan's animal cry as he clung desperately to the rigging.

"Told you," shouted Tom as the ship righted itself and they rolled in the last of the mainsail. "Piece of cake! Now let's get you back on deck."

Tom went first, calling encouragement to Dan as they made their way back down. Blood thumped in Dan's temples and his breath came in ragged gasps, but he'd done it. He'd done his job despite all his fears. A fierce feeling of exhilaration mingled with the last vestiges of terror as they finally reached the deck.

"Close-reef the foresail," called the captain.

Dan and Tom started forward but others were already scurrying up the shrouds of the foremast.

"Help out at the pumps, ye lazy waisters," yelled the bosun, swinging his knotted rope at the boys as they ran past him.

They took their turn at the handles, sweating as they cranked lines of heavy, water-filled buckets up from the bilges. Dan watched as they emptied onto the heaving deck, the water rushing out through the bubbling scuppers to the sea. The back-breaking work had been known to see men drop dead from exhaustion, and those toiling at the chain-pumps were relieved every ten minutes.

The bosun hurried down to check the water-level in the bilges. Dan and Tom were taking another turn at the pumps when he got back on deck.

"Three feet of water in the hold," he cried. "Keep pumping ye idle swabs. Do ye want us to sink? Keep pumping!"

They redoubled their efforts, the muscles in their arms screaming for rest, their lungs heaving.

"Baton down the hatches," called the captain, as another great wave crashed over the gunwales.

Men slithered across the sodden deck to cover the hatchways with sheets of tarpaulin, driving batons into the cleats to hold them down.

A great bang and the sound of splintering wood reached over the screaming of the storm.

"Loose cannon," roared the bosun, as sailors flung themselves out of the way of the madly careering gun.

It hurtled back across the deck and clanged loudly against another cannon. Men jumped forward, wrapping thick ropes around it and pulling it tight to the other gun. As the ship rolled again, they hung on, desperately holding the half-ton gun in place. More men ran to help and at last the cannon was secured.

"Is it lashed down?" called the first mate.

"Yes, sir," shouted the bosun.

"Take the names of the men responsible for securing it in the first place. We'll have *them* lashed as well."

The bosun's surly face broke into the semblance of a smile. "Aye Aye, sir."

As Savage mentally noted the names of the guilty gun-crew, Dan and Tom laboured on at the pumps, muscles aching as they struggled to keep their footing on the crazily pitching deck. A brilliant flash of lightning half-dazzled them as they forced their complaining arms to keep pumping, then the thunderclap rolled over them. Their ten minutes at the pumps felt like ten hours, and they collapsed on the deck as two others took their places. But there was to be no rest.

"Keep her bow on to the waves," the captain shouted at the helmsmen. "We're dead men if we turn beam on!"

He spotted Dan and Tom, prone on the deck.

"You two. This is no time to be lying around. Lend your strength to the wheel."

"What strength?" muttered Dan, but he forced himself to his feet and followed Tom up the bucking companionway to the quarterdeck.

The two helmsmen were fighting a losing battle to keep the ship on line. Dan and Tom threw their weight onto the helm and together the four of them forced the big wheel over, and they finally brought the reluctant ship head on to the waves. The captain lashed the helm in position then sent the breathless boys back to the pumps.

Flashes of lightning lit up walls of water towering over the ship, then she would be swept up to a peak before rushing down again into another trough. Dan mouthed half-forgotten prayers from his childhood and kept toiling at the pump, his spray-stung eyes never straying far from the churning maelstrom of the ocean.

The storm lasted well into the night then abated as suddenly as it had appeared. The men who had been taking turns at the pumps fell exhausted to the deck, the breath rasping in their throats. Too tired to climb the rigging and set the mainsail, they just lay there as the bosun laid into them with his knotted rope. Commodore Cavendish called him off and let the men rest, sailing on with only the reefed foresail moving them slowly through the now gently rolling sea.

Dan and Tom slept where they were.

The morning broke clear and bright, the sun large and red on the horizon. As it slowly spread its warmth across the deck, the boys slept on. Dan groaned as the bosun kicked him awake.

"Leake! Get up, ye lazy swab. Check the water level in the bilges."

Dan climbed painfully to his feet, his body aching all over, stiff and sore from a night spent on the hard deck and the toils of the previous evening. He unbattened the main hatch and hobbled down to the hold. The cold, rancid water came up to his knees.

"That was a close thing," said the bosun when Dan reported two feet of water in the bilges. "It was up to four and a half feet at one point. Any higher and we might have foundered."

Realising that he had sounded almost human, he turned on Dan.

"We nearly sank thanks to lazy lubbers like you and yer mate slacking on the pumps last night."

He half-heartedly swung his knotted rope at Dan as he turned away.

Hunger gnawed at Dan's stomach but the cooking fires had yet to be lit, and he had to content himself with a cold meal of sodden ship's biscuit. At least the water made it possible to bite into it. He gratefully accepted a mug of rum and, as it ran down his throat and warmed his belly, he allowed himself a tired smile and leant back against the lee rail letting the weak sun slowly dry his drenched clothes.

They'd come safely through the storm and anything was possible. Maybe he was born lucky. Perhaps he would find his dad after all.

CHAPTER 9

THE CHASE

Commodore Cavendish studied the ripped foresail, and the loose ropes and halyards that swung lazily from the mast. He called the bosun and gave orders for men to clear away the debris, secure ropes and sew damaged sails, before retiring at last to his cabin for some well-earned sleep.

Tom was busy with a needle and thread but Dan was having a welcome rest as the captain had, for once, excused the crew from holystoning for the day. A couple of unfortunates still toiled at the pumps and a few topmen worked in the rigging but otherwise the day was blessedly peaceful after the fury of the previous night. They sailed quietly on towards their meeting place.

The setting sun spread a warm glow over the cold Atlantic Ocean as they met up with the other ships. Both vessels were two-deck, fourth-rate ships-of-the-line but the *Advice* had a compliment of fifty guns to the *Norwich's* forty-six. They formed up line astern with the *Dover* at their head, as Commodore Cavendish was the Flag Officer commanding the small squadron.

Each vessel set lanthorns burning fore and aft, and the lookouts were doubled. They didn't want to lose one another, or worse collide, because a lone watchman had dozed off in the night.

Fortunately the weather was calm and the morning found all three ships still together. The captains held a Council of War on board the *Dover,* then they raised their mainsails and turned towards Cadiz to intercept the Spanish men-o-war.

The two boys swayed on the bowsprit, watching a pod of dolphins surf the ship's bow-wave below them.

"We're friends, Tom," said Dan. "Let's swear we'll never fall out again."

"You're right, mate. We've got to stick together."

"It's that girl," started Dan. "She's–"

"Don't talk about her!" snapped Tom, then forced a gentler note back into his voice. "If we don't talk about her then we won't fall out, will we?"

"Okay, but–"

"No buts!" We don't talk about her."

Dan admitted defeat and nodded his agreement.

"Ship ahoy!" came the cry from the mast head. "Dead ahead!"

The crew surged to the fore rails in a hum of voices. The wind had picked up and the bow plunged through the waves, sending sheets of spray over the men as the *Dover* sped on. They accepted their drenching as they eagerly scanned the horizon for the Spanish ships.

"There they are," shouted Tom, jumping up and down on the bowsprit. "There they are!"

He gestured wildly ahead.

Dan wiped seawater from his eyes and peered through the spindrift, but he could see nothing. More and more shouts went up and finally Dan spotted them. His heart raced. Three ships on the horizon. The enemy.

Men sprang into the rigging as the captain ordered all sails to be set, and the ship leapt forward.

The chase was on.

The excitement of the early morning dimmed as the pursuit drew slowly on. Blades had been sharpened, muskets cleaned and powder checked. Battle precautions could wait until they were closer to the enemy. Depending on the wind and the relative speeds of the ships, a chase could last for days, and the captain had no intention of depriving himself of his creature comforts. Not before he had to.

"Shall I beat to quarters, sir?" asked the bosun as the gap to the enemy ships slowly closed.

"Not yet, Mr Savage. It will be a long chase. Have the cook prepare something warm for the men. We'll get some hot food down them before we quench the cooking fires."

Commodore Cavendish stopped the bosun as he saluted and made to leave.

"Oh, and issue a full ration of rum to each hand. If they're going to die, they can do it with a merry head and a full stomach. Carry on."

"Aye Aye, sir."

Dan and Tom, empty mugs in hand, waited in the long queue leading to the barrel of rum. They smiled and rubbed their bellies, each enjoying the feeling of a stomach full of hot lobscouse – a salt beef stew with onions, potatoes and crushed ship's biscuit.

Whenever the *Dover* pitched forward, Dan could see the Spanish warships running ahead of them. They were considerably closer now.

"I wonder what it will be like," he said, the mug shaking slightly in his hand.

Tom had his eyes on the barrel of rum.

"It'll be great. I just hope there's still some left by the time we get there."

"Some Spaniards?"

"What are you on about? Some rum!"

"Oh!" said Dan. "I was wondering what the battle will be like. When we catch up with the Spanish."

"Don't worry about it," said Tom, licking his lips as he watched the quartermaster dish out yet another mug of rum. "It'll be fine. Piece of cake."

The queue grew smaller by the minute, but Tom still fretted. The quartermaster's ladle was getting worryingly near to the bottom of the barrel.

"W-we're getting close," stammered Dan, the big, Spanish men-o-war now filling his vision as well as his thoughts.

"Not close enough," sighed Tom, his eyes fixed firmly on the barrel.

Dan looked up at his friend, impressed, but not surprised, by his eagerness to get to grips with the enemy. He wished he felt the same way, but he was sure that his trembling hands and pounding heart would give away his true feelings.

He plucked up the courage to speak.

"I'm scared Tom," he admitted.

"Me too!"

Tom had eyes only for the barrel.

Dan gave a nervous laugh.

"Well I'm glad it's not just me. I just hope that I can take it."

"If you can't, I'll help you out."

They were nearly at the barrel now. Tom could almost taste the rum.

"You're a true friend Tom. You really are. I feel a lot better now."

Tom raised an eyebrow as he regarded his friend. Why was he making such a fuss over a mug of rum?

"It really isn't a problem Dan. Anything for a mate."

They reached the barrel and Tom sighed in relief as the quartermaster filled his mug to the brim. Dan took his share, and they moved forward to watch the chase.

With rum inside them, the sailors broke into a song, poking fun at the retreating enemy.

'Farewell and adieu to you Spanish ladies,
Farewell and adieu to you ladies of Spain,
For we've received orders for to sail for old England,
But we hope in a short time to see you again.'

More and more voices joined in, swelling the chorus.

'We will rant and we'll roar like true British sailors,
We'll rant and we'll roar all on the salt sea,
Until we strike soundings in the channel of England,
From Ushant to Scilly is thirty-five leagues.'

"Shall I shut them up, sir?" asked the bosun, swinging his knotted rope.

"No, Mr Savage," answered the captain. "Let them sing. Let them sing."

'Now let every man drink off his full bumper,
And let every man drink off his full glass,
We'll drink and be jolly and drown melancholy,
And here's to the health of each true-hearted lass.'

'We will rant and we'll roar like true British sailors,
We'll rant and we'll roar all on the salt sea,
Until we strike soundings in the channel of England,
From Ushant to Scilly is thirty-five leagues.'

As Dan listened to the seamen roaring out the chorus, he noticed the Spanish men-o-war. They weren't running any more. They hove-to, waiting for the British ships to close with them.

"Clear for action!" came a cry from the quarterdeck.

The singing stopped abruptly as drums and whistles filled the air. Men ran in every direction, some spreading netting above the open decks as protection from falling debris, while more was tied above the rails to deter enemy boarders. Topmen sprang into the rigging and waisters pulled out the tightly rolled hammocks and lashed them to the netting above the ships rails where they'd give some protection from musket balls. Others grabbed mallets and disappeared below.

The boys ran for the magazine. They passed men with mallets knocking down bulkheads to give more room to work the guns and to allow officers a clear view of each deck. They were also clearing away any wooden structures and furniture that could be turned into a lethal shower of splinters if struck by a cannonball. Everything was taken down to the hold or simply tossed out of the gun-ports.

In the galley the cook doused the cooking fires, and in the gun room the surgeon laid out the tools of his trade – his knives, saws, probes and forceps. Buckets of seawater stood ready to sluice blood from the makeshift operating table, between patients.

As Dan and Tom left the magazine they passed Henry Hall, who sneered at them as he scurried by in the opposite direction. Dan turned and scowled at his retreating back. *Yes you rat. I know where I'll find my mum's locket. And when I do…?*

"What's the matter with you," said Tom. "Get a move on. This is the real thing, not a drill."

When they got back on deck they found that the animal pens had been knocked down and thrown overboard. Captain Morgan screeched in the rigging as several goats and a pig ran around bleating and squealing with the ship's dog biting at their heels. Sailors chased after them and passed them down in slings into waiting boats. They would be towed safely behind the ship while it was in

85

action. Dan regarded them with ill-disguised envy etched in his tightly pinched face.

The pig proved hard to catch and missed the boat. When the sailors eventually caught it they just heaved it over the side into the sea. As the cannons were being loaded and primed, Dan watched the poor pig. It swam gamely for a while but soon fell behind as the warships surged on through the swell. It finally disappeared from sight.

Through all this organised chaos, hardly a word was spoken by the men as they had to be able to hear any orders called out by the officers.

"Mr Trimble."

The captain summoned his junior lieutenant.

"Escort my niece to the ladyhole."

The ladyhole was the safest place in the ship — a small triangular space deep in the hold where the hull supported the rudder, it was well under the water-line and out of range of enemy shot.

"M-my pleasure, sir," said Trimble, reddening slightly as he set off to fetch Emily.

With the Spaniards now stationary, the British squadron closed the gap rapidly, bows smashing through the waves under a full spread of canvas.

"Beat to quarters!" called the captain, and the drums sounded through the ship again.

Men disappeared down hatches and hurried to the heavy guns on the lower deck. Others ran to their posts on the upper deck. Marines, muskets loaded, lined the rails of the quarterdeck and the fo'c'sle. Still more climbed into the rigging and lashed themselves on so they could fire down on the Spanish when the time came.

Dan raced to the magazine again. He needed to have a cartridge ready to hand over as soon as the first shot had been fired, but it had to stay in its container. The safest place for the gunpowder was below the waterline in the magazine, not on deck where it could blow-up or set fire to the ship. Once the action started he would run for another.

He noticed that the sailors manning the big thirty-two pounders on the lower gun-deck, had wrapped thick neckerchiefs around their heads to protect their ears from the noise of the guns. They hardly needed to hear orders. Once the fighting started all they had to do was load and fire, for hour after hour until the engagement was over. After the first few broadsides they'd be half deaf anyway.

The cold December air chilled Dan despite the rum in his belly, but the gunners had all stripped to the waist. They obviously expected some hot work, and he'd heard that, if you were hit, the wound would heal better if there had been no cloth forced into it where it could fester. No man wanted the doctor probing about in an open wound, searching for fragments of clothing. Dan shuddered at the thought.

Commodore Cavendish called to the bosun. "Make sure the lower deck guns are double-shotted, Mr Savage."

The bosun hurried below, where the gun-crews rammed an extra cannonball down the barrels of their guns. At close range the double charge could deliver a devastating broadside.

"Upper deck guns, load with grapeshot," ordered the

captain.

Dan and Tom made trip after trip to the magazine, bringing up the canvas bags filled with small metal balls, and piling them by their guns. These bags would burst open when fired from the nine-pounder cannons, and spread a lethal hail of metal across the enemy deck. Grapeshot was a man-killer rather than a ship-killer, and was feared by all upper deck men.

With everything ready, Dan re-joined his gun-crew. The sponger and the loader stood by the muzzle. Next to them was the fireman with a bucket of seawater. It was his job to put out any fires that might start, and to keep the gun-barrel cool. Two sail trimmers, who spent most of their time in the rigging but helped to run out the cannon during action, crouched by the restraining ropes with two waisters. Scar towered over them all as, smoking linstock in hand, he planted himself by the touch hole of the gun.

And they waited for battle.

CHAPTER 10

BAPTISM OF FIRE

As they came into range, Dan could see the dark red and white of the Spanish flag fluttering defiantly at the stern of each ship. Suddenly the enemy disappeared behind a dense cloud of smoke. A roar like thunder rolled across the water and great splashes appeared in the sea ahead of the *Dover,* as the enemy's first salvo fell short.

"Make a note in the log," said the captain, as he sauntered up and down the quarterdeck. "Battle commenced, twelve noon, off Cape St. Vincent on the twenty-first of December in the year of our Lord seventeen hundred and nineteen."

The first mate scratched down the details, ready to be written up later.

Commodore Cavendish turned to the bosun. "We're in for a bit of a pounding before we can bring our guns to bear. Have the men lie down."

"Hit the deck!" shouted the bosun.

Marines and sailors flung themselves down in relief. Gunners crouched behind their cannons, hoping they would provide some protection from enemy fire. The officers remained on their feet. It would be unthinkable for a British officer to show any sign of fear in front of the men.

While the ships made their approach the Spaniards blasted them with broadsides but the British, still line astern with their bows facing the enemy, could only reply with the bow-chaser of the leading vessel. The captain didn't even bother to bring it into use.

"Bear off to the rear of the enemy. Two points to larboard," he called to the helmsman.

The new course saw them sailing diagonally across the face of the Spanish warships. They still presented a tempting target but at least now they couldn't be raked from bow to stern, where a single cannonball could travel the length of the ship causing mayhem and slaughter amongst guns and men.

The Spaniards began to get the range. They were firing on the up-roll of their ships and sending solid shot up into the rigging of the *Dover*, hoping to dismast her and put her out of action. Dan crouched lower behind his cannon and looked up in wide-eyed fascination as round-shot punched hole after hole in the sails. One cannonball fell short and bounced, skimming across the water. It hit the *Dover* on the waterline with a loud hollow thump. Luckily it was spent and failed to penetrate the thirty-inch thick, oak planking.

A strange whistling noise startled Dan.

"Chain-shot," said John Thatcher, half to himself.

Chain-shot consisted of two cannonballs joined with a length of cable. Its purpose was to bring down masts, which it did. The topgallant mast together with its sail disappeared overboard. Another chain-shot flew into the rigging, cutting a marine in two. His lower half landed next to Dan, the legs still kicking.

"He always liked to dance," murmured Thatcher.

"Heave that overboard," ordered the bosun.

Scar stepped forward and flung the twitching legs over the rail. The marine's top half still hung in the rigging, dripping blood and guts onto the deck below.

Dan rushed to the rail and threw up over the side.

They sailed on steadily towards the back of the Spanish line. Now only the rearmost ship could bring its guns to bear on the *Dover,* and the rain of iron reduced to a nagging drizzle. A fresh breeze helped as they covered the killing ground quickly and moved out of the line of fire. The *Advice* and the *Norwich* now became the targets of the Spanish gunners.

"Hard a starboard," cried the captain, and the helmsman brought the ship sharply about.

The topmen scurried around in the rigging, pulling in the studding sails as the wind came around onto the starboard beam. The *Dover* headed towards the windward side of the Spanish vessels as this would take the wind out of their sails if they tried to run. The Spaniards' defensive position now worked against them as the British had the advantage of manoeuvrability. The *Advice* and the *Norwich* fell in behind the *Dover*, and they closed on the enemy.

"God's wounds!" John Thatcher hammered his fist into the side of the cannon. "We're going to the windward of them. The larboard gunners will have all the fun. All we can do is crouch here while the Spaniards take pot shots at us. We'll have nothing to fire at."

"Let go the mainsheets," ordered the captain as they neared the first Spanish warship.

They needed to start slowing down now if they were to stop alongside their target, the man-o-war at the far end of the line. With no time to furl the sails, the topmen just let them loose where they snapped and flapped madly in the freshening breeze. The *Dover*'s momentum carried her remorselessly on towards the waiting enemy.

The first Spaniard loomed ahead. The *Guadalupe*. The fifty-eight gun two-decker towered over them as they approached. They were so close that Dan could see the cursing, bearded faces of the Spanish sailors. As they caught up with her, the British tars gave a great roar and the Spaniards jumped as if they'd been hit by a broadside.

The enemy guns began to fire one by one as they came to bear on the *Dover*. Bits of wood flew from her bows as heavy cannonballs tore through her thick timbers and into the soft flesh of the men behind. A round-shot smashed through the bulwark of the upper deck, sending out a lethal shower of wooden splinters that scythed down three men on the larboard side. Six men from the starboard watch ran over and carried them down to the surgeon. When they returned they were ordered to stay and serve the depleted larboard guns.

Dan tried to swallow but his mouth was too dry. His hands shook as he took a drink from the fireman's bucket. He quickly spat it out again. *Salt water*! As more men fell,

Dan crouched between the guns, trying to make himself as small as he could. Still the British held their fire.

As the quarterdeck came level with the stern of the Spaniard, a round-shot hit the first lieutenant full in the chest, plucking him from his feet and hurling him over the starboard rail and into the sea.

"Mr Trimble," called the captain as he strolled along beside the weather rail. "Take over as first mate, if you please."

When they were completely alongside the enemy warship, the order came at last.

"Fire!" shouted the captain.

"Fire!" echoed the bosun.

"Fire!" yelled the bosun's mate stationed on the lower gun-deck.

A huge roar rent the air as twenty-five guns spat death at the Spaniards. The whole ship seemed to jump back with the power of the broadside. Smoke obscured the *Guadalupe,* but Dan knew the shots had hit home when the agonised screams of dying men pierced through the thick gun-fog.

The cannons crashed back against their restraining ropes and the spongers leapt to the muzzles, the water hissing and steaming as they rammed wet sponges down the barrels to kill any burning embers that could ignite the next charge prematurely.

The *Dover* sailed on towards the *Tolosa,* where twenty-eight double-shotted cannons waited for them. Sweat pouring from them, the larboard gunners desperately pushed powder cartridges down barrels and rammed them into place as the ship came up alongside the Spaniard. But before they could load with round or grapeshot, the Spanish broadside hit them with a sickening crash.

Dan looked on in horror as the deck became a slaughterhouse. Arms and legs, torn off by round-shot, skittered across the planks. Foot-long wooden splinters lodged in soft flesh. Grown men, shredded by grapeshot, screamed for their mothers. Bloody bodies twitched in the rigging while others lay unmoving beside the shattered barrels of their cannons.

Heart pounding, Dan peered desperately through the smoke trying to see if his friend was alright, but Tom was nowhere to be seen.

The *Dover* sailed on by without reply as the surviving gun-crews rammed round-shot or grape down the barrels of their cannons. Men from the starboard watch ran across to take the place of dead larboard gunners.

They slowly closed on the last Spanish vessel, the *Hermiona,* a three deck, fifty-two gun warship.

Advice and *Norwich* would take care of the other two ships. *Hermiona* was the *Dover's* prey.

This was to be *their* adversary.

Their battle.

CHAPTER 11

A TEST OF NERVE

The Spanish Flagship's stern and forecastles towered over the *Dover* as it came alongside, allowing her marines to sweep the British deck with musket fire. Commodore Cavendish ignored the whining bullets as they peppered the quarterdeck around him.

"Back sails," he cried, and the *Dover* slowed to a crawl.

Both captains held their big guns in check, waiting until a full broadside could be brought to bear.

The seconds ticked by like hours.

"Fire!" yelled the captain.

With a deafening roar, both ships' broadsides erupted together.

A jet of blood hit Dan in the face as Lieutenant Trimble's mangled body landed at his feet, then everything disappeared in a thick fog of grey smoke. As it drifted away, Dan could see one of the British gunners writhing on the deck, his intestines spread around him. The bosun shouted orders and two of his shipmates picked up the screaming man and heaved him overboard to drown.

"Leake!"

Dan could see the bosun's lips moving but could hear nothing. Everything had gone eerily quiet after the broadside, and the swirling smoke and the strange silence gave the whole gory scene around him a surreal feel. He stared at the bosun, trying to make sense of his angry hand signals. He shook his head to clear it.

"Leake!"

Dan's hearing began to return, and he ran over to the furious bosun.

"Your gutless mate's disappeared. Kelly needs a new powder monkey."

Dan stood in shock for a moment.

Tom! What's happened to Tom?

"Move!" shouted the bosun, pushing him violently towards the larboard guns.

In a daze, he stumbled over to Sam Kelly as he prepared to fire his cannon.

"Where's Tom," Dan yelled. "Where's Tom?"

"Not seen him since the first broadside. We need powder. Now!"

As he spoke, Sam put a smouldering linstock to the cannon's touch-hole, and the gun hammered back as it blasted death at the Spaniards.

Gathering his wits, Dan ran for the hatch. Before he could duck into it, a round-shot passed so close that the shock wave knocked him from his feet. He found himself staring at the headless body of a powder monkey, the lifeless hands clutching an empty cartridge case.

'Tom!' his half-stunned mind screamed at him.

With a gasp of relief he realised the body was too small

to be Tom's. He grabbed the dead boy's container and scrambled to the hatchway.

He made his way down into the bowels of the ship, eyes darting around, looking for any sign of his friend. The lower deck was so full of gun-smoke that he could see nothing as he hurried past, but he could hear the heavy guns thundering away as the gunners fired as fast as they could, no longer bothering with broadsides. Each gun-crew now fought its own deadly battle with the Spanish gunners opposite. In the race to load and fire, second place would be rewarded by death.

He reached the magazine and hurried down into the darkness. As he grabbed a powder cartridge he thought he heard a low moan. He sensed rather than saw movement under the stairway.

"Who's there?" he whispered.

No answer, just the low moan again.

He raised his voice. "Who's there?"

"Is... Is that y-you, Dan?"

He scrambled over.

"Tom, are you alright? Are you injured? Tom! Speak to me!"

Tom's voice was barely audible.

"I... I'm n-not hurt."

"Then what are you doing down here?"

"It's the noise, Dan. The c-cannons. I can't take the noise. It's quiet down here. I thought I'd s-stay for a while. Until it quietens down."

"You can't stay here!" shouted Dan. "We're in the middle of a battle. They'll hang you if they find you hiding below deck."

"Just for a while Dan. I can't go up. Not yet."

"Don't you understand?" yelled Dan. "They'll hang you! Come on. Let's go!"

Tom didn't move.

Dan's mind raced. *He had to get powder up to Sam Kelly, but how could he leave Tom down here?*

"Tom!"

He shook his friend.

"I've got to go. The guns need powder."

"Don't leave me, Dan."

"I have to!"

Tom still held his empty canister. Dan thrust the dead boy's container into his other hand.

"Fill those with cartridges. You can do that, can't you?"

"Y-yes. I guess so."

"I'll come back for you. Just fill the canisters."

Dan half-dragged a reluctant Tom from the stairwell and over to the cartridges, then he dashed up the steps.

Out on deck lethal showers of metal flew back and forth, but Dan was hardly aware of them.

He had to get his friend out of the magazine, but how?

Dan threw a powder cartridge to Sam Kelly, and then moved back towards the hatch. A musket ball splintered the deck at his feet, and he looked up. Spanish marines, lining *Hermiona's* high stern and forecastles, kept up a steady stream of fire into the *Dover*, but they were mainly aiming at the officers on the quarterdeck. He could see Commodore Cavendish sauntering up and down amidst the hail of fire as if he was out for a Sunday stroll.

"Is he down there?"

The bosun's contorted face came out of nowhere and stopped inches from Dan's.

"Is that cowardly toad skulking down below?"

Dan thought fast.

"He's filling the canisters and I'm bringing them up. It's quicker that way."

"Like hell it is," snapped the bosun. "If that gallows' dodger isn't up here in the next five minutes, I won't wait for the hanging. I'll shoot him myself. Clear?"

The cannon next to them jumped as it took a direct hit from a round-shot. The loader shrieked as the heavy gun toppled over, trapping him by his legs.

"Yes Bosun. That's clear. He'll be here."

Dan ran past the screaming gunner and heaved himself down the hatchway.

Tom was as good as dead unless he could get him out of the magazine.

"Here!"

Tom, held out two canisters as Dan hurried in.

Dan took one but left his friend with the other. He quickly filled the third container.

"Come on," he urged. "Let's get these up to the guns."

"I'm not going up there. I'm alright where I am."

"No, you're not. If you stay here they'll hang you."

Tom hesitated. "Maybe later."

"Not later. Now!"

Tom didn't move.

Dan's brain raced.

He had to get Tom out of there. He had to make him see

reason.

"There are people dying up there, Tom," he shouted. "Your shipmates are dying because they can't shoot as fast as the Spaniards as they don't have enough gunpowder. They don't have enough powder because of *you*. They're dying because of *you*. Are you going to skulk down here and let them die?"

Tom trembled.

"I... I guess not."

"Then come on!"

Tom still hesitated so Dan took him by the arm and dragged him to the stairway.

"You can do this Tom," he urged as he pushed him up the steps. "I'm right behind you. I'll be with you all the way."

They made their way up painfully slowly, but eventually reached the hatchway. As they looked out over the bloody carnage of the upper deck, Dan felt Tom tremble beside him.

"You feed the first cannon then get back to the magazine," shouted Dan over the roar of the guns. "I'll do the far end."

Tom swallowed hard, then crawled out onto the bucking deck. He scurried over to the nearest gun and threw his cartridge at the gunner. The bosun glowered after him as he dived back down the hatch.

Dan slithered over the blood-soaked deck as quickly as he could. He thrust a cartridge into Sam Kelly's hands then passed another to the loader of the next cannon.

From the corner of his eye he could see Sam struggling

to push the charge down the barrel as he tried to fight the gun on his own. The rest of his crew lay dead around him. As he rammed the charge down the muzzle, a huge flash lit up the ship and Sam disappeared, blown to pieces as the gun went off in his face. In his hurry to fire the gun he'd forgotten to sponge out the hot barrel, and burning fragments from the last cartridge had ignited the powder as he rammed it home.

Shaking, Dan lurched back to the hatchway. He met Tom coming the other way.

"You won't say anything, will you?" begged Tom. "I mean, about how you found me down there. It was the noise. I froze. But I'm all right now."

Tom took a deep breath and then, tight-lipped and trembling, he heaved himself out onto the deck and ran to the guns.

Dan nodded to himself, then stumbled down to the magazine for more gunpowder.

CHAPTER 12

SHOT AND SHELL

As the battle thundered on, the surviving powder monkeys now outnumbered the undamaged guns. Dan spotted Henry Hall cowering behind the mainmast, safe from enemy fire.

This was the cowardly rat who'd stolen his locket.

With the rage of battle already on him, Dan exploded. He dragged the trembling boy out from his place of shelter.

"Thief!" he screamed in his face. "Where's my locket?"

"What locket?" squealed the skinny powder monkey, shaking like a loose halyard in a gale.

"Where is it?"

"I don't know anyth–"

"Thief!" yelled Dan, grabbing him by the lapels.

As he shook him, a round-shot took Henry Hall's head from his shoulders. Dan stared in horror then dropped the bloody body to the deck. Half in shock, he scrabbled through the twitching boy's pockets looking for his locket. He found nothing.

"Robbing the dead now are ye, Leake?"

The bosun loomed over him.

"That's despicable, even for you."

"No, I—"

"Save yer excuses for yer court martial," growled the bosun. "Right now, get some water to the lower gun-deck. They're dying of thirst down there."

He kicked Dan towards the bow.

As the red mist lifted, Dan began to shake.

What had he done?

After a brief argument with the marine guarding the water butt, Dan filled a bucket and, in a trance, made his way down the stairway. Smoke swirled out of the lower gun-deck as the big guns fired away with a constant *thump, thump, thump*. He dipped his handkerchief in the water then hesitated, unsure whether to cover his ears or his mouth. After a second he wrapped it over his mouth before plunging on into the murk.

In the dense smog, Dan could see no more than a yard in front of him. He reached the first cannon and called out, but no one could hear him. The sound in the low-beamed room was indescribable. Guns roared; cannonballs smashed through timber and flesh, and clanged off metal; and throughout it all the British sailors cheered at the top of their voices.

Stripped to the waist, sweat running down their powder-blackened bodies, the gunners loaded and fired their cannon, too busy to notice him.

Finally the gun-captain looked around. Dan held up the ladle and mimed drinking. The gunners raced over and crowded him, greedily slurping down the water, not waiting for their turn with the ladle but plunging powdergrimed fists into the bucket and drinking from their hands.

"Bless you," one of them mouthed, then they went back to their grim duty at the gun.

Down at this level the ships were nearly touching and, as the air briefly cleared, Dan could see the Spanish gunners through the open gun-port. He could have reached out and touched them. The gun fired and smoke obscured his view again.

He hurried on to the next crew. A little powder monkey, no more than eight years old, scurried past too close as the gun as went off. The cannon recoiled violently and knocked the boy to the other side of the deck where he lay still. The men ignored him as they drank thirstily.

Dan made his way doggedly onward, slipping and sliding in blood, guts and vomit, as he tried to keep his feet and reach the next gun-crew. Things had been bad enough up on deck but down here it was a scene from hell. The living fought on amongst the dead and dying. Severed arms and legs lay strewn about the floor. Blood and bits of brain stained the ceiling and walls. Several cannons had their muzzles sheared off as they fought their bloody, point-blank battle with the Spaniards. Throughout it all the British gunners fired and cheered, fired and cheered, in a deadly, relentless rhythm.

Relief flowed over Dan when a parched sailor drained the last of the water, and he was finally able to escape the carnage of the lower gun-deck. His eyes streamed and he coughed up smoke as he climbed up to the fresher air of the upper deck, where he bumped into his friend. Tom still wasn't his normal, cock-sure self, and he flinched each time the guns fired, but he was doing his duty.

Before they could speak, Commodore Cavendish hailed them from the quarterdeck. They expected some rebuke but instead the captain shouted encouragement.

"Hot work, eh lads? We're giving them a pounding. We've got bigger guns and we're firing faster. It's simple mathematics. They'll have to strike."

He meant that they'd have to haul down their flag and surrender the ship.

"Carry on lads, you're doing well."

Tom seemed to straighten a little at the officer's words. "Captain!"

The helmsman pointed astern.

Commodore Cavendish turned to see the *Advice* limping away from the engagement, her mainmast gone. Her opponent, the *Tolosa*, rather than pursuing her victim, piled on sail and steered for the *Dover*.

"Starboard guns, make ready!" called the captain.

The Spanish warship quickly closed the gap and hove-to alongside. Dan bit his lip. *This wasn't good.* Now they were fighting a battle on both sides at once.

The Spaniards fired first but the *Dover's* starboard guns were still double-shotted, and they ripped great chunks from the *Tolosa*. On the upper decks the grapeshot from the British ship caused far greater carnage than the round-shot of the enemy. The gun-crews reloaded and fired in a steady rhythm honed by hours of practise. British gunners could keep up a faster rate of fire than any other nation.

On the larboard side, the enemy guns had fallen silent. Tom grabbed Dan's arm and pointed at the *Hermiona*. Her lower-deck gunners had abandoned their cannons and were now swarming up to join marines and sailors at the rail. Spaniards threw grappling hooks onto the *Dover* and pulled her tight into *Hermiona's* deadly embrace.

"Prepare to repel boarders!" yelled the captain.

Men ran for cutlasses and boarding pikes but the Spaniards, swords in hand, were already leaping over the rails or swinging onto the deck from ropes lashed to the rigging. The British sailors fought back with anything that came to hand. Some battered at the Spanish with ramrods. Others stabbed or clubbed at them with the handspikes used to turn and aim the cannons.

The British fought like lions, but they were steadily forced back as more and more Spaniards swarmed aboard. The bulk of the *Dover's* crew still laboured below decks firing shot after shot through wreaths of smoke at an enemy who was no longer there, but was seething onto the deck above.

"Come on Dan!"

Tom grabbed a heavy belaying pin from the gunwale and, using it as a club, leapt into the middle of the Spaniards. Dan looked desperately around for a weapon and spotted a handspike on the deck. He picked it up and ran after Tom who was fighting like a madman, battering at the enemy with his makeshift cudgel. Dan joined him, crouching low and stabbing at legs with his handspike.

"This is more like it," roared Tom, laying about him with the belaying pin. "This is proper fighting."

In the chaos of the fierce hand-to-hand combat, Dan and Tom found themselves forced away from their comrades.

A group of Spanish sailors advanced on them with boarding pikes, followed by a marine brandishing a bayonet-tipped musket.

As they retreated from the stabbing points, Dan felt the fo'c'sle wall hard against his back. His eyes darted around but they were on their own. The Spaniards outnumbered them three to one and there was nowhere to run. They were trapped.

A huge, bearded sailor stabbed at Dan with a pike. He jumped to the side but the point caught his sleeve and pinned him to the wall. He despairingly jabbed back with his handspike, but he didn't have the reach. Trapped and helpless, he looked to Tom for aid but his friend was fighting for his life against three men, and losing the battle. Blood seeped from several cuts on Tom's left arm as he tried to ward off his attackers.

The pike-man kept Dan pinned to the wall as the smiling Spanish marine stepped forward and drew back his bayonet for the fatal thrust. Dan said a silent prayer and braced himself for the agony to come.

Suddenly the marine's skull cracked open like an egg as Scar appeared, mallet in hand. He backhanded the pike-man with a huge fist before smashing yet another enemy to the deck with the wooden hammer. John Thatcher, roaring like a bull, rushed by swinging a ramrod, and knocked a Spaniard from his feet. Tom rallied and despatched one of his tormentors with a blow from his club. The last man turned and fled as the rest of Dan's gun-crew dashed in.

But the main body of Spaniards still advanced.

A great shout went up as the starboard gunners, realising

the danger, abandoned their cannons and raced across the deck, tearing into the Spaniards, slashing and stabbing with cutlasses and pikes. The Spanish shuddered to a halt but stood their ground and fought back. They still outnumbered the British.

A body of marines jumped down from the fo'c'sle into the waist, hammering their rifle butts into enemy faces and stabbing with bayonets whenever they got enough room. A quick-thinking gunner on the quarterdeck grabbed the swivel-gun and fired grapeshot into the hoard of Spaniards lining *Hermiona's* rail, ready to board. The chance of reinforcement from the Spanish ship disappeared in a welter of blood and gore. The boarding party wavered but still fought on.

The fight hung in the balance but then the lower-deck gunners, shouted up from below by a bosun's mate, came screaming out of the hatchways and flung themselves on the Spaniards, stabbing, hacking, kicking and biting. The enemy wilted under the savage attack then, assaulted on three sides, they turned and fled back over the rail, jumping for the safety of their own vessel. One man missed his footing and fell between the ships. He struggled to the surface only to be crushed as a swell closed the gap between the two hulls.

The British gave a shout of triumph as the last of the Spaniards jumped from the *Dover*, a hail of missiles following him over the rail.

The gunners raced back to their cannons, and the steady pounding began again. Joseph Brown's wife had taken over as powder monkey for his gun, so Dan stayed with the depleted larboard watch. With enemy ships on both sides, the *Dover* was only just holding its own. Men were falling like nine pins, bowled over by the heavy Spanish cannonballs.

Behind them the *Norwich*, wallowing and obviously holed below the water-line, had also disengaged. The *Guadalupe*, rather than chase what appeared to be a sinking ship, left her to her fate and sailed on to join the attack on the *Dover*.

Commodore Cavendish saw the danger. He noticed the Spanish ship manoeuvring to bring its broadside to bear on the *Dover*'s near defenceless stern. If that happened she could rake the British vessel from stern to bow and the ship would be lost.

"Make all sail," called the captain. "Look lively now."

Sailors rushed up into the rigging, ignoring the musket fire of the Spanish marines. The heavy bullets hit a few, sending them crashing down to their deaths, but the rest stuck to their task and soon had the sails set.

But the ship didn't move. *Hermiona*'s grappling hooks held her fast.

"Cut those ropes," cried the captain. "Sharpish or we'll be raked."

Tom had his blood up now, and the fear that had paralysed him earlier had melted away in the heat of the battle. He grabbed an axe and ran to the larboard rail, closely followed by Scar and three others. Enemy musket fire now concentrated on them as they slashed at the heavy cords with axes and cutlasses. A blast of grapeshot swept three men from the rail but Scar and Tom still survived. They ignored the musket balls buzzing around them like angry hornets, and hacked away the remaining grappling irons.

As Tom chopped at the last cable it finally parted, and they slid free. They were pulling away, but painfully slowly because the *Tolosa* was windward of them and stealing their wind. The *Guadalupe*, which had already built up its speed, closed rapidly and prepared to sail across the stern of the *Dover*. They were nearly clear of the *Tolosa* and the *Hermiona,* but time was running out.

They were going to be raked.

"Hard a starboard!" shouted the captain, and the helmsman threw himself at the wheel, swinging the ship into the *Tolosa.*

The stern of the *Dover* collided with the bow of the Spanish vessel spinning it around clockwise, using it as a shield, just as the *Guadalupe* fired her broadside. The hail of iron slammed into the Spaniard's sister ship and left the *Dover* almost unscathed.

"Hard a larboard!"

The *Dover* straightened up and, catching the wind now that she was free of the *Tolosa's* sails, she quickly picked up speed and headed after the fleeing *Advice* and *Norwich.*

The wind had strengthened alarmingly and the damaged Spanish ships didn't risk giving chase. They contented themselves with the knowledge that they had taken on a British squadron and put them to flight.

On board the *Dover*, Philip Cavendish retired to his cabin and hung his head. He had done what was needed to save his ship from falling into enemy hands, but that wouldn't hold much weight with the Admiralty. He had been defeated. He had fled from the enemy and he would be lucky not to face a court martial. He plotted a course for Gibraltar then stood at the big stern window, staring out at the billowing waves, and cursing Cape St. Vincent, all Spaniards, and the captains of the *Advice* and the *Norwich*.

Dan and Tom helped throw the last of the dead overboard and then, not bothering to sling their hammocks, lay down where they were and fell into an exhausted sleep on the blood-soaked deck.

CHAPTER 13

TRUE COLOURS

Dan had been up since dawn clearing the debris of battle: cutting away smashed rigging, throwing broken timbers and severed limbs overboard, and washing blood from the deck. Visions of yesterday's horrors kept springing unbidden into his head. Tom had returned from the surgeon who'd stitched up the cuts on his arm. They worked in silence, still mentally and physically exhausted.

A rhythmic thumping came from below decks as carpenters hammered in wooden bungs where cannonballs had punched through the ship's timbers. Other men toiled at the pumps to clear the water that had built up in the bilges. As the boys swept the deck the bosun's eyes followed them, a malicious scowl on his brutal face. He made his way to the grand cabin.

"What's the butcher's bill, Mister Savage?"

The captain's face was drawn and lined, and he still wore his blood-spattered clothes from the day before. His long, white wig lay on the desk in front of him revealing a short stubble of dark hair.

"One hundred and fifty-four killed or wounded, sir."

"Good grief, that many?"

Philip Cavendish rubbed his greying temples.

"It's worse than I feared."

"That's for all three ships, sir," said the bosun.

"Well I suppose that's something. Thank goodness for small mercies."

"Mrs Brown lost a hand helping out on her husband's gun. He's asking if she's due any compensation, sir."

The bosun's scowl showed what he thought about that idea.

"I'll tell him 'no' of course, but I promised that I'd ask you. The man was blubbering like a child. She was comforting *him*!"

"I'll write to the Admiralty, but I'll be surprised if they grant her anything. She's not on the ship's muster."

The captain's face creased into a frown.

"No doubt they'll criticise me for having a woman on board."

"Yes, sir. They're nothing but trouble."

"That's not what I meant," snapped the captain.

"No, sir. Me neither."

Philip Cavendish glared at the bosun for a second, then slumped back in his chair.

"And the damage to the ship?" he asked.

"Nothing the carpenters can't deal with, sir. She's seaworthy and the mainmast is sound. We should make it to Gibraltar without trouble."

"Thank you, Mr Savage," said the captain, dismissing him.

But the bosun stayed where he was.

Commodore Cavendish looked up wearily.

"Was there anything else?"

"I'm sorry to have to report a case of cowardice, sir. Desertion in the face of the enemy."

The bosun did not sound sorry.

"Hanging offence!" he added hopefully.

The captain sighed. "The man's name please, Mister Savage?"

"Boy, sir. It was Tom Bailey."

"Tom Baaailey," the captain drawled slowly, trying to place the name.

"The stowaway, sir."

Commodore Cavendish fixed the bosun with a hard stare.

"Would that be the same Tom Bailey I saw jumping into the middle of the Spanish boarding party with nothing but a belaying pin for a weapon?"

"Yes, sir, but—"

"The same Tom Bailey who stood by the rail and cut the ship free when half the Spanish navy was using him for target practise?"

"He did, but—"

"I'll tell you something, Bosun. If the rest of you had half the courage of young Tom, we'd have won that battle."

"But sir, I—"

"I don't want to hear any more about this matter, is that clear?"

"Yes, sir."

"Dismissed!"

"And I caught Dan Leake robbing a—"

"Are you deaf, Mister Savage? I said, 'dismissed'!"

"Yes, sir."

The bosun saluted smartly then marched from the cabin, murder smouldering in his dark eyes.

Emily approached the boys as they worked. She stood for a moment, looking sadly at the blood-stained planking.

"I missed it all," she whined. "I was stuck in that hold all day. It was hell."

Dan bit down his fury.

All those men had died, and she was angry that she'd missed it? She didn't know what hell was, but he did. He did now.

"Hi Emily," said Tom.

She ignored him. "Hello Dan," she purred.

Dan carried on sweeping.

"I need to talk to you."

Dan said nothing.

"Please Dan, there's something I have to say."

Dan sighed and allowed himself to be led to a quiet spot by the fo'c'sle. Tom remained where he was, glaring after them, and attacking the deck with his broom.

"What do you want?" snapped Dan, stepping back and crossing his arms.

"Why are you ignoring me these days?"

Again Dan didn't reply.

"You know I like you," she simpered.

Dan hesitated.

"I thought you liked Tom?"

Emily laughed, throwing back her long, blonde hair.

"That great oaf? No, it was always you I liked."

"Tom's not an oaf and anyway, I don't like *you*!"

Dan turned half away.

"Why not? I'm pretty, aren't I?"

She tilted her head to the side and treated him to her best smile.

"I know you think I'm pretty."

"I used to," snapped Dan. "But now I know that you're not."

The smile disappeared.

"I saw you," Dan went on. "I saw your face when that man was being flogged. You were enjoying it."

"Well, of course I was. He'd attacked you and he was getting what he deserved."

"No one deserves that!"

"And I was curious," she admitted. "It gets so boring on this damned ship. I feel like I'm going out of my mind, cooped up in that cabin all day. At least it was something to do."

"Something to do?"

A vein twitched in Dan's neck.

"I'd not seen a flogging before."

A faint smile brushed Emily's lips.

"It was interesting."

Dan forced himself to breath slowly.

"A man having the skin torn from his back. You think that's interesting?"

"Don't *you*?"

The disbelief in Emily's voice was genuine.

"No I don't. I'll tell you what I think. I think you're evil."

The pretty face transformed in a second, the mouth tightening and the eyes narrowing to slits.

"So you don't like me?"

She looked like a snake, a coiled snake ready to strike.

"No, I don't like you."

Dan watched her scowling mouth and the cold eyes that blazed ice at him.

"And I think you're ugly."

He meant it.

"You'll be sorry you said that," she hissed. "I'll make you sorry."

Her hand shot out and slapped his face. As she hit him, a silver locket fell out of her sleeve and landed at Dan's feet. He stared at it in disbelief then snatched it up. Emily didn't even notice.

"I'll tell you something else I've never seen."

Her voice was calm again. Icily calm.

"I've never seen someone hanged at sea. I'd like to see that. In fact I'd like to see *you* hang, Daniel Leake. And I will."

She slapped him again then opened her mouth and screamed.

Dan stood frozen, as Savage and the bosun's mates pounded over.

"He attacked me," she screeched, pointing at Dan. "I overheard him and his friend plotting mutiny. He hit me and told me he'd slit my throat if I said anything."

Dan laughed nervously.

"She's not serious."

"Yes I am! He attacked me."

The bosun's mates seized Dan and pinned his arms behind his back. Two more took hold of a bewildered-looking Tom.

A cold smile spread slowly over the bosun's weather-beaten face.

"You've done it now, Leake! You'll swing for this. You and your mutinous mate."

Tom shook his manacles, his fists balled tight.

"What the hell did you do?"

"I didn't do anything."

The stagnant stench in the bilges assailed Dan's nostrils, making him wretch.

"It's Emily. She's evil. I've been trying to tell you, but you wouldn't listen. It was her who stole my locket."

And he'd accused Henry Hall. He'd as good as killed him.

Dan struggled for breath. No fresh air reached this far down into the ship. Dead rats floated in the murky water that lapped at his feet, and live ones scurried over his legs. He remembered Sam telling him that the men working down here had no time to go to the heads and just relieved themselves where they stood. He tried to pull his feet out of the fetid liquid, but they were shackled tight to the floor.

Footsteps sounded on the gangway. Dan turned his head as the bosun came up to them. He'd never seen him looking happier.

"Are ye enjoying yer new accommodation then lads? It's not much but it's home, ain't it?"

"Why are we here?" demanded Tom. "We haven't done anything."

"Ye've been plotting mutiny and ye've assaulted the cap'n's niece."

"We have not!"

"And ye deserted yer post in battle, didn't ye Bailey? Ye might have fooled the cap'n, but ye didn't fool me. Ye deserve to swing for that if nothing else."

Tom fell silent, his eyes downcast.

The bosun turned to Dan.

"Ye needn't worry, Leake. They don't hang admirals."

His sudden laugh barked out in the quiet of the bilges.

"Mind ye, there's worse things than hanging. They could give ye a hundred lashes. Ye'd die after about sixty, but us poor souls still have to flog away at yer dead body till ye've had the full hundred. I'll tell ye, it's a hard life being a bosun."

Dan shuddered as he thought of John Thatcher's flogging.

And he'd only received two lashes. What would a hundred do to your back?

"Keel-hauling. Now there's a proper punishment. I'd love to see the pair of ye keel-hauled."

The bosun looked for a reaction from the boys but got none.

"So ye don't know what keel-hauling is then? They tie ropes to yer arms and legs and throw ye over the side face down. The men then drag ye along the bottom of the ship

119

and pull what's left of ye up from the other side. Trouble is the keel's covered in barnacles, and they take the skin off yer back. If ye open yer mouth to scream, then ye'll drown. When ye start bleeding, then it gets interesting because the blood attracts sharks. Many's the time I've seen the ropes come back up with only the arms and legs attached. If they keel-haul both of ye then pray ye go first. The sharks will be waiting for the next one. Lickin' their lips, they'll be."

The bosun ruffled Dan's hair as he sat, pale-faced and shaking.

"But don't worry, Leake. They say the cap'n prefers a good hanging."

A cheerful smile, and he was gone.

Philip Cavendish looked searchingly at Dan. The startling blue eyes were steady and unblinking. The boy was telling the truth.

"He hit her," said the bosun. "Saw it with my own eyes, I did. And mutiny. That's a hanging offence, sir. Says so in the regulations."

"At sea, Mister Savage, the captain's word is law, is it not?"

"Yes, sir."

The bosun smiled.

"Ye can hang man or boy on yer own authority."

"And I believe that I, not you, am captain?"

The bosun's face fell.

"Yes, sir."

"So I think I will decide for myself who I hang, and who

I do not."

"But he hit her! Saw it with my own eyes."

"Mister Dawson here saw it with his own eyes as well. He tells me it was my niece who struck the blows and that Leake didn't raise a finger."

The captain stared down the bosun.

"So which is it that you're questioning, Mister Savage, the midshipman's eyesight or his word?"

The bosun's face turned puce as he glared at the sixteen-year-old midshipman.

"Neither, sir. It was a bit dark and it all happened so fast. I could have been mistaken."

"Yes, you could."

Dan felt a surge of hope.

The captain regarded Dan and Tom.

"You don't strike me as mutineers. You did your duty well when we took on the Spaniards."

"Thank you, sir," said Dan. "We're not mutineers. We volunteered."

"Yes, you did, didn't you?"

The captain stroked his chin as he looked at the boy before him. If he didn't punish him he would be calling his niece a liar, and she would be seen as the evil viper that he suspected she was. But what to do?

He turned to Tom.

"Master Bailey, there is no evidence against you. You're free to go."

"Thank you, sir."

Tom glanced anxiously at his friend as he left.

Commodore Cavendish considered Dan thoughtfully.

"But my niece did not strike you for no reason. You must have given her some offence?"

"Yes, sir. I may have insulted her."

"Would you care to elaborate?"

Dan didn't know what 'elaborate' meant.

"No, sir."

"Very well."

"Shall I have him lashed, sir," asked the bosun eagerly.

He could see now that there would be no hanging, but a flogging was nearly as good.

The captain ignored him.

"I can't have the ship's boys insulting ladies. You understand that, don't you, Leake?"

Dan nodded.

"But what to do with you?"

"We could have him keel-hauled, sir," suggested the bosun, his hands clasped under his chin as if in prayer. "It's a long time since we had a good keel-hauling."

"That's because it's a barbaric practise."

"Yes sir, properly barbaric. Shall I tell the men to prepare for a keel-hauling?"

Ignoring the bosun's eager advice, Commodore Cavendish stared out of the big, stern window, his eyes on the darkening horizon.

"Mister Savage, I believe there's a bit of a squall coming up. It should hit us this evening, don't you think?"

"Yes, sir."

"I think we'll have him mast-headed. A night in the rigging in a gale should cool him down a bit and teach him some manners. Have him spend the night at the masthead.

Carry on."

"Aye Aye, sir."

Savage was smiling again.

"Come with me, Leake."

As they left the cabin the bosun leant down and whispered in Dan's ear.

"Ye don't like heights, do ye Leake. Before the night's out ye'll be wishing they'd hanged ye."

CHAPTER 14

MAN OVERBOARD

The storm hit them like a punch in the face. Dan reeled on the madly heaving deck and gaped up at the men clinging to the rigging as they frantically reefed the sails. Rain hammered sideways into him, and the wind shrieked like the tortured ghosts of the sailors lost at Cape St. Vincent.

"Ye'll be up there in a minute, don't worry," the bosun shouted over the howling wind. "We'll wait to see if it picks up a bit first."

Waves crashed onto the deck as the ship pitched violently, and water piled up against the bulwark before gushing out of the scupper holes. Four men struggled to hold the wheel steady in the swelling sea. A sudden flash of lightening lit up the night and Dan could see the ocean towering above them as they slid into a trough. Then the thunderclap rolled over them.

"Alright, Leake. Up ye go."

The bosun pushed Dan into the rigging.

Dan glanced up at the wildly swinging mast, and gulped. With a shudder, he began to climb. "Don't look down, don't look down," he repeated to himself as he crawled slowly up, his feet scrabbling to get a grip on the rain-soaked ratlines. He reached the crow's nest and made to pull himself in through the lubber hole.

A voice bellowed up from below.

"You're not a landlubber any more. Climb in through the top like a sailor."

Dan's heart sank. Up to this point the rigging had slanted in towards the mast, but now it angled outwards. To reach the top he'd have to climb out backwards before scrambling over and into the crow's nest. It would be hard enough on a calm day, but in this wind…? *He didn't stand a chance.*

He reached out and got a good grip with both hands then walked his feet up the mast until he could hook them through the rigging leading to the crow's nest. Slowly he crawled out backwards. The ship rolled and he found himself gaping down at nothing but sea as he hung on, his nerves screaming like the wind in the sheets. After an age, the ship righted itself, but Dan was too scared to move. He steeled himself. *He couldn't just hang there until his strength gave out.* With a huge effort of will he began to climb, but his feet slipped from the rigging and he swung wildly in the air. Finally his flailing legs found the foot ropes again and he scrambled up to the top of the masthead, letting out a huge sigh of relief as he dropped into the crow's nest.

The platform rocked violently. Dan lashed himself to the swaying mast with a loose rope. He had been warned that he could be swept off the masthead if he fell asleep.

Securely tied to the mast, Dan settled in for a long, cold night.

The storm raged on unabated. The moon showed occasionally through the scudding clouds, but mostly nothing interrupted the pitch black of the night. The wind howled about him but Dan could sometimes make out the rhythmic chanting of the men working the pumps below. The battering seas had opened up the hasty repairs to the hull and, although the hatches were battened down, the waves sweeping over the decks still found their way into the hold. Half the crew were up fighting a desperate battle to empty the water out faster than it came in.

The cold cut through Dan's sodden clothes and ate into his bones, but pure fatigue saw him dozing off until another great gust threw him sideways. The securing rope snapped him awake and he yelped in terror as he found himself staring straight down into the black of the ocean before the ship hauled herself upright again. He wanted to move around to keep warm but, when he tried to stand, he was thrown off his feet as the ship plunged one way then the other, so he huddled down and clung to the mast.

The sails had been close-reefed and the *Dover* was now running with just the spritsail set. They needed this much to make headway and keep bow on to the swell, or risk capsizing. The crow's nest jerked about as the night drew slowly on. Battered and bruised, Dan could do nothing but endure.

Dan awoke with a start. He couldn't believe he'd actually fallen asleep. It was dawn but the sky was so dark he could hardly tell. The wind had calmed a little but still battered the ship, throwing it around in the heaving sea. Hanging on to the lip of the crow's nest he cautiously peered over. The deck was almost deserted, but he could see two men at the helm, and Tom and Scar toiling at the pumps. Most of the crew had been up all night fighting the storm and the captain had finally allowed the exhausted men to go below for some sleep.

"Leake!"

It was the bosun.

"Fun time's over. Get yer backside down here. There's work to be done."

Dan slowly unlashed himself from the mast. He could hardly feel his fingers they were so cold. He climbed painfully to his feet, every muscle aching, then started down the lubber hole.

As soon as his leg appeared the bosun shouted.

"Not the lubber hole. Ye climb out the top like a proper sailor."

Down on deck Tom watched anxiously as his friend timidly lowered himself over the side of the crow's nest. Dan clung on as a strong gust hit the ship then, taking a deep breath, he stretched down with his legs, searching for a foothold. He missed and his feet scrabbled on thin air. Dan gripped the ropes tightly as he tried again. His foot caught but then slipped off, and he swung out over the sea as the ship heeled under another icy blast of wind. He clung on desperately but his frozen hands were losing their grip. His heart thumped his chest like a prize fighter pummelling a punch bag. Eyes wide, he stared at the angry sea boiling beneath him, then his left hand slipped from the rope. Hanging by one arm he despairingly tried to hold on but felt his fingers weakening.

Don't let go! Don't let go!

The gale carried away his scream as he lost his grip and plummeted down into the raging ocean.

"Man overboard!" yelled Tom, but the shrieking wind plucked the words from his mouth and spun them away.

The bosun smirked, and did nothing. Scar, stripped to the waist, leapt into the heaving waters.

Tom looked around in despair. The ship's boats had been smashed in the battle. He spotted an empty water butt and rolled it to the side of the ship then, grabbing a length of rope, he hefted the barrel over the rail and jumped after it. The water hit him with an icy slap that took the wind from his lungs. Gasping in air he called out, "Dan! Dan!"

There was no reply.

Tom kept calling out as he lashed himself to the barrel. He heard a splashing beside him and Scar appeared, towing a half-conscious Dan. Scar took the rope and tied Dan to the barrel as he spluttered and coughed himself back to life. Tom waved and yelled at the ship until he was hoarse but only the bosun had seen them go overboard, and he hadn't sounded the alarm.

Thoughts crowded into Dan's head as he clung to the barrel.

He was going to die and what had he achieved? He'd proved he could stand and fight, but they'd lost the battle. All he'd managed to do was kill Henry Hall, an innocent boy. His real enemies, Emily and the bosun, had won and now he was going to die. As for his friends, Tom and Scar,

he'd be the death of them as well. And he'd never see his
father again. It had all been for nothing.

He watched in helpless resignation as the *Dover* sailed slowly out of sight, and they found themselves alone in the endless, churning ocean.

CHAPTER 15

THE DEVIL AND THE DEEP BLUE SEA

The storm finally passed and the waters fell into an eerie calm. Dan looked around in dismay. Nothing but ocean. Fear gripped him in an icy embrace as cold as the biting sea. Scar shook him by the arm, and began kicking through the water.

Dan understood.

"We have to swim," he called to Tom. "We have to keep moving."

"We're in the middle of nowhere," cried Tom. "What's the point of swimming?"

"If we don't move, the cold will kill us."

Dan started kicking his feet.

"Why bother?" said Tom. "We've had it anyway."

"Then why did you jump in after me?"

"Because I'm an idiot, that's why."

Beside them, Scar swam on strongly. Tom sighed and joined in.

"And I thought the ship would stop," he added.

Dan spluttered and spat out a mouthful of seawater.

"I don't think they even knew I'd gone overboard."

"The bosun knew. He saw you fall, but the toad-spotted beef-wit didn't raise the alarm."

A flush of anger warmed Dan briefly but the icy water soon cooled him down again. He knew in his heart that Tom was right. They couldn't survive for long. The cold would kill them if they weren't picked up soon, and the chances of that were small. The storm had carried them out of the main shipping lanes, and now they were alone in the middle of the Atlantic.

He began to worry about the dark water beneath him and what might be in it. He tried desperately to think of something else, and his mind turned to his father. Despite everything he'd always felt that somehow he'd find him, but now...?

He'd failed. He was going to die here and he'd never see his dad again.

Dan started violently as something brushed against his leg. *Shark,* screamed his brain. His head whipped one way then the other as he frantically scanned the ocean around him.

"What is it? What's wrong?" yelled Tom.

"There's something in the water!"

They looked around, wild-eyed, waiting for a fin to break surface.

Nothing happened.

"You imagined it," said Tom.

"No I didn't. Something touched my leg."

"Well, whatever it was, it's gone now," Tom reassured him.

But his eyes continued to dart around as they kicked

131

themselves along again.

Scar swam on silently at their side.

A cold despair crept over Dan as night fell. Clouds obscured the moon and the darkness filled his soul. He could not see his friends, but could hear the rhythmic splashing as they swam on. Weariness overcame him, and he drifted into sleep only to have Scar shake him roughly awake. He began kicking his legs again, terror of the black, bottomless ocean helping to keep his eyes open. Twice more he fell asleep and twice more Scar shook him awake. The morning found them half-dead from cold and exhaustion.

"Dan! Dan!" shouted Tom.

"What? Where?"

Dan's eyes jerkily searched the dark waters, the blood hammering in his temples.

"Behind you!"

He spun around in panic, trying to spot the fin he knew must be there.

"A sail," yelled Tom. "I can see a sail"

Dan raised his eyes and there it was. A ship not more than a league away.

"Over here," they called again and again, waving frantically.

"They can't see us," groaned Dan, shoulders slumping. "Three heads in the ocean. They'll never spot us down here."

Scar untied himself from the barrel and somehow climbed top of it. Dan and Tom struggled to hold it steady as the big man stood up, waving at the ship. The boys shouted their lungs out.

"They're turning," cried Tom. "They've seen us."

As the big brig came steadily towards them, the boys cheered madly, but Scar silently noted that it flew no flag and that it sailed high in the water. So it carried no cargo. It was no merchantman.

The ship hove-to and sent out a skiff to pick them up. It took four men to pull an exhausted Scar into the boat, then two sailors dragged Tom over the stern, quickly followed by Dan.

"What are you doing out here?" one of them asked.

"I'm looking for my dad," said Dan.

"Well you're not going to find him in there, are you?" the man laughed.

Dan didn't mind. He lay in the bottom of the boat, exhausted and elated at the same time.

They were going to live after all.

They reached the brig and the seamen helped them up the side. The crew gathered around to stare. The boys looked back happily, just enjoying the feeling of having a solid deck under their feet and glad to be alive. Scar studied his surroundings more carefully. He noted the rows of cannons on the deck and the fact that there must be at least seventy men aboard, far more than needed to sail a ship of this size.

A tall, handsome man, smartly dressed in yellow and red striped calico breeches and matching coat, pushed through the crowd. Sharp grey eyes regarded them from under a black tricorn hat.

"I'm John Rackham," said the man, as if the name should mean something to them. "Calico Jack?"

When they still didn't respond his tone became darker.

"I'm the captain of this ship, and we don't normally pick up flotsam. Who are you?"

Tom spoke up. "We fell overboard from a man-o-war."

"So you're sailors, are you? Fighting men?"

"Yes, sir." confirmed Tom.

Calico Jack stroked his recently shaved chin and nodded slowly.

"We might find some use for you then. We'll not waste food and water on anyone who's no use to us. What are your names?"

"I'm Tom Bailey."

"And I'm Dan Leake."

The captain turned to the huge man standing silently beside the boys. He raised an eyebrow when the man didn't speak.

"He's called Scar, sir," said Dan. "He's a mute."

Calico Jack frowned.

"We've no room for mutes on this ship. Throw him overboard."

As Dan stood in stunned silence, two men started forward. A growling sound came from the back of Scar's throat, and they both stopped. One paused, looking anxiously from his captain to the huge, scowling man in front of him. The other, a wiry, ginger-haired man with a wooden leg, showed no hesitation. He stepped back.

"*You* throw him overboard."

The captain drew a pistol and pointed it at the giant.

Scar regarded him coldly for a second, then seemed to make up his mind.

"Algernon Lynch," he said in a deep booming voice.

The boys stared at him wide-eyed, then gawped at each other.

"He can speak," gasped Dan.

"His name's Algernon," gasped Tom.

Calico Jack lowered his pistol. "So you've found your tongue, have you? And what use can you be to this ship, Algernon Lynch?"

Tom snorted.

"Topman and gun-captain," growled Scar. "Ten years at sea."

"Experienced sailors are always welcome. Would you be willing to sign on with us? Sign the *Articles*? You know what we are, don't you?"

"Scar know what you are. And yes, he sign."

"What does he mean?" Dan whispered. "What are they?"

"I've no idea," admitted Tom. "But make sure you sound like you'll be useful to them. I don't fancy going back in that water."

The captain's voice cut across them.

"And you ... Tom, was it? What can you do for us?"

"Eight years at sea," Tom lied. "Powder monkey and topman."

"Powder monkey *and* topman?"

The captain raised an eyebrow as he studied Tom's round, honest-looking face.

"That's an unlikely combination. Let's see you up in

the rigging."

Tom scampered easily and quickly up to the masthead and back down again.

"Okay," admitted the captain. "You look like a topman. Are you willing to sign the *Articles*?"

"Yes, sir," said Tom quickly, still not knowing what they were. "I'll sign."

The captain turned to Dan. He didn't look impressed as he studied the small, shivering boy in front of him, although Dan was now wirily strong from the constant toil on the man-o-war.

"And what about you, Sprat?"

"I'm a powder monkey," said Dan.

"We've just signed one of those on."

The man's voice darkened.

"We don't need another. What else can you do?"

"Nothing!" sighed Dan.

"Don't be stupid," hissed Tom. "Say something. Anything."

"I can read and write," Dan blurted out.

"God's wounds!"

Calico Jack laughed out loud, pointing Dan out to the rest of the crew.

"It can read and write."

They burst out laughing, and Dan reddened and sank back into himself.

"You're no use at all then," said Calico Jack. "But you make me laugh. Personally I'd keep you on, but it's up to the men. It's their decision."

Dan glanced at the crew who glared back without pity.

"But you're the captain," he pleaded. "They have to do what you say, don't they?"

"We're a democracy. We vote on what we're going to do. No man's another's master aboard this ship."

Calico Jack pointed at Scar and called to the men.

"Crewmate or shark bait?"

"Crewmate!" came the shout.

He pointed at Tom.

"Shark bait or shipmate?"

"Shipmate!" was the answer.

"And what about the sprat?"

The captain, flicked a thumb towards Dan.

"He's useless, but I say he stays. What say you?"

The crew huddled together, coldly discussing Dan's fate. A stocky, evil-looking man with a patch over one eye, stepped forward.

"We send him back where he came from," he shouted.

"Cork?" asked Dan hopefully.

Calico Jack laughed again.

"No. The sea," snarled the one-eyed man. "We throw sprats back, don't we?"

"Aye!" shouted the crew.

Dan looked around in panic, desperately searching for a friendly face in the baying mob. A slim, good-looking young sailor, a spotted red and white bandana on his head, stepped out in front of him.

"You're from Cork, are you? I was born there myself. We'll have to get together and talk of old times."

The sailor turned to the crew.

"You'll vote him on board, or answer to me."

The one-eyed man stepped forward, drawing his cutlass.

"The men have voted," he spat. "Now stand aside, Bonny. Get out of my way!"

The slim young sailor pulled out a long, sharp-bladed knife.

"Put down your weapon Jim Price, or I'll put *you* down."

With a snarl, the man leapt forward, chopping viciously with his cutlass. The young sailor danced out of the way, bringing up the knife and severing the man's windpipe in one neat swipe. Jim Price collapsed to his knees, clutching at his throat and gurgling on his own blood as it pumped out through his fingers. He slowly pitched forward and lay still.

"It looks like we've got a vacancy," said the young sailor, pointing the bloody knife at the wide-eyed crew. "Now vote this lad on board."

The decision was unanimous.

Calico Jack looked on dispassionately as two men tossed Jim Price's lifeless body overboard. It bobbed beside the ship, blood seeping into the gently rolling water, then suddenly the corpse whipped from side to side in the jaws of a huge shark. Dan looked on in horror as two more sharks joined in the feeding frenzy and the waters around them boiled as they thrashed about tearing lumps from the corpse. He shuddered. They had been in those same waters minutes before. That could have been him, or his friends.

"Bosun," called Calico Jack, unconcerned with the fate of a dead body. "See that the new men get something to eat and drink, and some dry clothes, then bring them to my cabin to sign the *Articles of Agreement*."

A big man with a bull neck and long, black hair hanging over heavily muscled shoulders, stepped out from the crowd. Dan looked down expecting to see a knotted rope in the bosun's gnarled fist, but it was empty.

"George Featherston," the man said, holding out his hand.

"Dan Leake," murmured Dan, taking it.

"Welcome aboard the *William*. Could you all do with a tot of rum?"

Tom's head nodded vigorously.

"I'm Tom Bailey."

The bosun shook Tom's hand. Big as he was, he had to look up as he shook hands with Scar.

"Fetch some dry clothes for the lads," he told one of the crew then studied Scar doubtfully. "And a blanket for the ogre. I'll not have him splitting a pair of my breeches."

Feeling warmer now in dry shirt and trousers, Dan sat on the deck with his friends, eating a meal of ship's biscuit and lightly cooked fish. To Dan's guilty disappointment, Tom now wore clothes that fitted and no longer looked comical. Scar tapped his biscuit on the deck and a number of weevils dropped out. Dan and Tom glanced at each other, then quickly followed suit, Tom bashing his biscuit so hard that it disintegrated.

"What are these *Articles* they want us to sign?" Dan asked Tom.

"Scar tell you what they are."

Dan jumped. He wasn't used to the big man speaking.

139

He had to ask the question.

"Why didn't you talk on board the *Dover*? Why did you pretend to be mute?"

"Story keep. Need listen now. Lives depend on it."

"Sail ahoy!" cried a lookout from the mast above them, cutting off Scar's tale. "Off the starboard bow."

Calico Jack hurried onto the quarterdeck and studied the horizon through his spyglass. Dan could feel the quivering tension as men crowded the starboard rail, trying to catch a glimpse of the other ship.

"Bring her about," called the captain. "Set all sail. And run up the flag."

A great roar went up from the crew as they leapt into the rigging and unfurled the sails. As a chasing wind filled them, the ship surged forward, the prow coming around towards the distant vessel. Men grabbed cutlasses and ran to the bow, vulture-like eyes fixed on the small ship ahead of them.

Dan and Tom looked up as the colours were hoisted. They gasped in horror as a black flag furled out in the wind. On it, set above crossed swords, a death-white skull grinned down at them.

Eyes wide, Dan turned to Tom.

"Pirates!" they both mouthed silently.

Dan's eyes remained on the flag, but his thoughts were elsewhere. *He'd tried to find his dad, and he'd failed. Instead of running into his father's arms, he'd be walking the plank into the cold embrace of the sea.* His hand closed tightly around the silver locket at his neck as his head slowly sank to his chest.

HISTORICAL NOTE

Dan, Tom and Scar are fictional characters but Commodore Philip Cavendish, His Majesty's Ship *Dover,* and the *Battle of Cape St. Vincent* are real. The punishments and practices described did occur in the Royal Navy at the time, and the food that they ate is pretty much as it would have been.

It was also common for cooks to have missing limbs as it was considered an easy job for sailors maimed in battle. Whether or not they could cook hardly came into it.

Typical interview for an 18th Century ship's cook:

Captain:	*"How many limbs have you got?"*
Sailor:	*"Three. I lost an arm at the Battle of Cape Passaro."*
Captain:	*"I think you've got the makings of a good cook."*
Sailor :	*"And I lost an eye!"*
Captain:	*"When can you start?"*

The *Battle of Cape St. Vincent* took place on 21 December 1719 in the *War of the Quadruple Alliance* (Britain, France, Austria and the Dutch Republic against Spain). Three Spanish men-of-war, *Tolosa*, *Guadalupe* and *Hermiona*, drove off three Royal Navy warships, *Dover*, *Norwich* and *Advice*, under Commodore Philip Cavendish, inflicting heavy damage and losses on them. The defeat did not end Philip Cavendish's career as he feared. He went on to become an admiral.

In the book I have Dan and Tom in separate watches. In reality this would have meant that they wouldn't have seen much of each other as one watch would be working while the other was sleeping or relaxing. I conveniently overlooked this because, for dramatic effect, I wanted some separation between the two boys, but not to the extent that they would not see each other.

Dan's rescuers, Calico Jack and his crew, were real life pirates, and will appear again in *Hoist the Black Flag*, the second book in *The Adventures of Dan Leake* trilogy.

HOIST THE BLACK FLAG

The following pages contain the first chapter of *Hoist The Black Flag*, the second novel in the trilogy *The Adventures of Dan Leake*.

CHAPTER 1

THE PIRATE CODE

The loud boom of a cannon jolted Dan Leake awake. He looked around in confusion, then remembered where he was. As he wiped the sleep from his eyes, Tom and Scar tumbled from their hammocks, stretching and cursing. After their ordeal, adrift in the sea, the few hours of rest they'd had wasn't nearly enough, and they were all still dog-tired. But at least they were warm, dry and, more importantly, alive.

Grabbing his jacket, Dan reluctantly followed his friends up on deck. A small merchantman lay ahead of them, a Dutch flag flying from her stern. The bow-chaser of the *William* fired again, putting a shot across the bows of the other vessel. But, instead of heaving-to and striking her colours, the ship's stern-chaser belched smoke, and a cannonball whistled over their heads.

"She wants a fight," yelled Calico Jack. "Let's give her a broadside before we board. Hard a starboard."

"Aye Aye, Captain," called the helmsman as he swung the *William* around to bring her larboard guns to bear.

Behind the gunners, row upon row of howling men

waved cutlasses and pistols, screaming curses at the terrified sailors scurrying around on the merchantman.

By Dan's side, Tom Bailey stared wide-eyed at the black flag that had been hoisted at the *William*'s mizzenmast. A death-white skull grinned down at them from its bitter perch on a pair of crossed swords.

"Pirates!" he whispered. "I can't believe we've been picked up by pirates."

Dan regarded the big, blond lad beside him. Tom was his best friend. Along with their gun-captain, Scar, Tom had jumped into the sea to try and save him when he had fallen overboard from His Majesty's Ship *Dover*. But the smirking bosun had ignored their cries for help and the ship had sailed on, leaving them alone in the wide Atlantic Ocean. Their joy at being plucked from the sea had been short-lived. They'd soon discovered the true nature of their rescuers.

"I'm sorry, Tom," sighed Dan. "I should never have got you involved in this."

When Dan's mother had died, he'd persuaded Tom to run away to sea with him, hoping to find his father who'd been pressed into the Royal Navy years before. It seemed like only yesterday that they'd shared their fifteenth birthday aboard the *Dover*, but now it looked as though they would never see their sixteenth. Saved from a watery grave only to find themselves at the mercy of a bunch of murderous cutthroats.

"I'm sorry," he said again.

"What do you mean, 'sorry'?"

Tom's saucer-wide eyes darted from the Jolly Roger to

the howling pirates.

"This is great!"

Dan sighed again. Tom loved a fight, but he rarely stopped to think of the consequences.

All of a sudden the merchantman's flag fluttered to the deck, cut down by one of its crewmen. The ship turned into the wind and drifted to a stop.

"Hold your fire," called Calico Jack. "We don't want to damage anything valuable."

The launch and jollyboat, loaded with jubilant, well-armed pirates, set off towards the other vessel under the protective cover of the *William's* guns. Dan, Tom and Scar were amongst the boarders, the captain testing their loyalty as the newest, albeit reluctant, members of his crew.

They reached the merchantman and scurried up the side like hungry cockroaches. The sailors offered no resistance. Half of them were English, and they pointed to the Dutch captain who they'd trussed hand and foot on his own quarterdeck.

A small nervous man spoke up. "It was him who f-fired on you," he stammered. "We b-begged him to surrender and refused to help him with the g-gun, but he fired it himself. He was g-going to fire again, but we st-stopped him."

Calico Jack looked down his nose at the sailor. "So, there's only one brave man amongst you is there?"

The small man seemed to shrink even further. "B-but w-we..."

"Still, I can't have anyone thinking they can fire on Calico Jack and live to tell the tale, can I?"

He strode over to the cannon.

"Is it loaded?"

"Y-yes, sir. Apart from the ball."

A chain-shot, two cannonballs joined with a length of iron cable, lay by the muzzle of the gun.

"So, Captain." Calico Jack doffed his black tricorn hat to the man bound-up on the deck. "You want to fire the cannon again, do you? Well I won't disappoint you. Scar!"

The big man pushed forward.

"Help the captain up, if you please. Stand him next to his gun."

Scar effortlessly lifted the man to his bound feet.

"Hold him there." Jack turned away. "Thackeray!"

A fat, old pirate, nearly fifty years of age, hobbled up to them.

"Tie the noble captain to the chain-shot."

The Dutchman blanched but said nothing as his legs were firmly attached to the chain by a stout length of rope.

"Load!" called Jack.

One pirate eased the cannonballs, which were welded to either end of the chain, into the barrel of the gun. Another picked up a ramrod and forced them down.

The captain began to shake.

Calico Jack picked up a still-smouldering linstock from the deck and blew on the end. He passed it to the terrified captain.

"Fire when you're ready, sir."

The trembling man looked pleadingly into Jack's hard face but, when he saw no mercy there, he straightened up.

"Damn Je naar de Hel!" he shouted, and held the linstock to the touch hole.

The cannon erupted with a deafening roar and the captain was snatched from the deck. Dan watched in horrified fascination as the screaming man flew a quarter of a mile before plunging after the chain-shot and disappearing beneath the waves.

The merchant seamen trembled, one of them throwing up over the side. Even the battle-hardened pirates stood in stunned silence.

"Wow," said Tom, bouncing on his toes as he watched the ripples die away. "That was grea..." He saw the look on Dan's face. "...gruesome. Really gruesome."

Calico Jack smiled at the captured crew as he strutted up and down in his striped calico jacket, his silver-buckled shoes glinting in the bright sunshine. "I need some volunteers," he said.

Every man took a step back.

Jack didn't bat an eye. "Is there a carpenter aboard?" he asked. "Our ship needs a carpenter."

The small seaman pointed out a tall sailor with short, ginger hair that stood to attention over a hang-dog face. "John Howell's a carpenter."

Howell scowled at him.

"Well John, are you willing to follow a new captain, or would you rather follow your old one?" Calico Jack looked pointedly out to sea and patted the cannon.

John Howell swallowed hard. "I'll follow you."

"Good man. I also need a decent cook."

A slim young man of about nineteen stepped forward.

His short, black hair sat above a prematurely lined, weather-beaten, but not unpleasant face. His dark eyes were unflinching as he spoke.

"My name's Mark Read and I'm a cook."

Calico Jack looked him up and down. "A good cook?" he asked.

The young man puffed out his chest. "The best. Had my own tavern in Holland in better times."

"What were you doing in the Low Countries?" asked Jack with interest. "Have you served in the army?"

"I was a soldier once," he admitted.

"Then you're welcome aboard the *William* As long as you're willing to sign the *Articles of Agreement*."

Dan frowned. There was that term again. Calico Jack had mentioned it when they'd been pulled from the sea, but then he'd been distracted by the sight of the merchantman and Dan and his friends had been allowed to rest after their ordeal in the ocean.

"I'll sign," said the young man.

His shipmates glared at him, bristling with disapproval.

"That's all the men I want," said Calico Jack. "I don't need the rest of you." He tapped the cannon as he spoke.

The sailors began to wail in English and Dutch, shouting each other down in their newfound enthusiasm to join the pirate crew.

Jack held up a hand for silence. "Don't worry," he said gently. "You're going to live. I want you to remember the name, *Calico Jack*. Tell people what you saw today. If a crew surrenders to me then they'll live. But if any man fights me, he will die, and he won't die easy. You can even keep your ship. This heap of woodworm and barnacles would only slow me down. All I want is your cargo."

The sailors slumped in relief.

Jack's eyes flashed with greed. "Now what is your cargo?"

"Bricks. Bleedin' bricks," complained McKaig, a wiry, one-legged Scotsman. "What the hell are we meant t' dae wi' bricks? Jack's useless."

"Aye, you're right for once," agreed Thackeray. "Jack Rackham may be bold but he's unlucky. What plunder have we had since we voted him captain?"

"Just bleedin' bricks," snarled McKaig. "We might as well have Charles Vane back as captain. He wasnae brave but we still took some silver in his time, no' just bleedin' bricks. By my reckoning we..."

The Scotsman stopped in mid flow, his ginger hair bristling.

"What do ye mean, 'right for once'? Ye'll get my foot up yer arse if ye dinnae watch it!"

"Aye, maybe I would," growled Thackeray. "If it was still attached to yer leg!"

"Take that back ye slack-bellied, bilge-rat!"

Calico Jack sauntered onto the deck. He had some of the bricks loaded onto the *William* as ballast, indifferent to the grumblings of the crew. He approached Dan as he stood alone considering the cruelty he'd witnessed earlier.

"Why the dark looks, Master Sprat? Are you another one who doesn't like bricks, or is something else eating you?"

Dan had promised Scar he wouldn't say anything, but he couldn't help himself. "That poor man! How could you do that to him? You're nothing but an animal. You're a monster!"

"A monster am I? Tell me Master Sprat, how many men did you kill when you were aboard a British man-o-war?"

"I... I only..."

"Twenty? Thirty? More? You were a powder monkey. How many cartridges did you bring to the guns? How many times did they fire? How many men died?"

"But... but they were the enemy."

"They were still human beings and you sent them straight to hell, didn't you?"

"I was just doing my duty."

Dan loosened the collar of his shirt. *He had done nothing wrong. And yet this pirate was somehow making him feel guilty.*

"And what of *my* duty, Dan. It's my duty to find plunder for the crew and to try and keep them alive while I do it. How many men did you say you killed?"

Dan remained silent. *He had done nothing wrong.*

"I killed *one* man," said Jack. "One! His death may have looked horrific - it was meant to - but his sacrifice will save many lives. Word will get around that Calico Jack is a ruthless, brutal murderer, but will show mercy to anyone who surrenders their cargo without a fight. How many lives will that save in the future? Even more than you've *killed*, I'll wager. Who is the monster, Dan? You or me?"

He straightened up, then strolled back to the grand

cabin, leaving Dan deep in thought.

Still angry and confused by his conversation with Calico Jack, Dan confronted Scar. When he'd first met him, Dan had been terrified of the gigantic, scar-faced black man, but he had taken the young Irish lad under his wing. He'd never said why. In fact he'd never said anything. They had thought Scar was a mute, but he had shocked them by speaking when the buccaneers had pulled them from the sea – the first words Dan had ever heard him utter.

"You knew didn't you?" Dan glared at the giant. "You knew they were pirates!"

"Scar knew. But better pirate than drown."

"I'd rather have taken my chance in the sea," snapped Dan.

"What chance?" boomed Scar, then pointed to the rail. "If you want swim with Jim Price, then jump."

After they'd been rescued, Price had wanted to throw Dan back into the water but, on hearing that he was from Cork, a slim young Irishman had stepped between them. When Price raised his cutlass, the smaller man had drawn a knife and slit his throat in one, blistering movement. The crew had tossed the body overboard without a second thought. Dan remembered the sharks dismembering the bloody corpse, and he shuddered. Caught between the Devil and the deep blue sea, he sank into a sullen silence.

"Sulk later," growled the big man. "Not much time. Listen now if want to live. Scar tell about *Articles*."

The boys said nothing so Scar went on. "*Articles* are pact between captain and crew. If sign then you pirate and

153

hang if captured."

Dan, folded his arms across his chest. "And if we don't sign?"

"They slit throat. Throw to shark. Life to them little value. Dan already see."

They sat in silence for a minute, Scar letting his words sink in.

Tom looked up at the huge man. "What are *you* going to do?"

"Scar sign. If ship captured, Scar say pirate force him. Hope they believe."

"I'll not sign," said Dan through clenched teeth. "I'm not going to be a pirate. You saw what they did to that poor man. They're animals."

Tom frowned. "Don't be stupid! You heard Scar. We've got to sign."

"I'm here to find my dad. He's in the Royal Navy. What would he think if he heard I'd become a pirate? What if he's in the ship that captures us? He'd have to hang his own son. I can't do that to him. I can't let him down."

"You're not going to find your dad if you're dead," snapped Tom. "Sign the *Articles*."

"No!"

The bosun, a big man with a thick neck and broad shoulders, called them over. Remembering his time in the navy, Dan glanced down at the man's brawny arms, half-expecting to see a knotted rope in his gnarled hands, but they were empty.

"Ye've to come to the captain's cabin," he said, and led them to the stern.

154

"You have to sign the *Articles*," Tom hissed.

Dan shook his head.

As they entered the cabin, Calico Jack rose from behind a big, mahogany desk. Gaudily dressed in yellow and red striped calico breeches and matching coat, he dominated the room with his height and mere presence. Sharp, grey eyes regarded them from under a black, tricorn hat.

"Ah, gentlemen," he said, taking off his hat and running a strong hand through the long mane of straw-coloured hair that framed his handsome, almost feminine face. "I have the *Articles of Agreement* here."

He tossed his hat on the desk, reached over and pulled a sheet of paper from under a large, white paperweight. Dan recoiled. It was a human skull.

"I know the sprat can read, but what about the rest of you?"

Dan reddened, remembering the pirates' laughter when he told them that he could read and write.

"I'm not a sprat," he snapped.

"Well, well," said Calico Jack, smiling. "A sprat with spirit. I like that."

He handed the sheet to Dan.

"Read it to your friends please, Master Sprat."

Dan snatched the paper, glared at the pirate, then began to read aloud.

"One. The Captain is to have two shares of any plunder; the Quartermaster is to have one and a half shares; the Mate, Gunner and Bosun, one and a quarter shares; the men, one share; boys, half a share.

"Two. He that shall be found guilty of cowardice in the

155

time of action shall be marooned with a bottle of water, powder, pistol and shot.

"Three. If any plunder is not delivered to the Quartermaster in the space of twenty-four hours, the culprit shall suffer what punishment the Captain and the majority of the Company shall think fit.

"Four. He that should lose a limb in time of engagement shall have the sum of six hundred pieces-of-eight. One hundred for an eye or a finger.

"Five. He that shall be guilty of drunkenness in time of engagement shall suffer what punishment the Captain and majority of the Company shall think fit.

"Six. Lights and candles to be put out at eight o'clock at night. If any of the crew after that hour still remain inclined for drinking, they do it on the deck.

"Seven. Each man shall keep their pistols and cutlass clean and fit for service.

"Eight. No striking one another on board, but every man's quarrels to be ended on shore with sword and pistol."

Dan looked at the captain. "No striking one another on board? What happened on deck this morning, between Jim Price and that Irishman?"

"That one doesn't abide by the rules," said Calico Jack ruefully. "Now let's get the *Articles* signed."

He picked up a quill and dipped it in an ink pot on the desk.

"Algernon Lynch," he called.

Tom snorted. He'd only just found out that Scar's real name was Algernon. It didn't fit well with the big man's fearsome appearance.

Scar withered Tom with a look, then stepped forward and made his mark.

Calico Jack nodded to the human skull on his desk. "Swear you'll abide by the *Articles*."

Scar wrapped a massive hand around the skull and swore the oath.

"Tom Bailey!"

Tom took the quill and made his mark, then swore his oath on the skull.

"Dan Leake!"

Dan didn't move.

"Sign the *Articles*," hissed Tom. "They're decent rules, aren't they?"

"I'll not be a pirate," said Dan, his voice loud in the wooden cabin.

Tom groaned.

The captain regarded Dan coldly. "So you don't like our company then, Master Sprat? We can soon remedy that. You can go back to swimming, if you like? Sign the *Articles of Agreement*."

"No! I'll not be a pirate."

"Then tell me what use you are to us. How do I justify taking food from other mouths to feed you? You told me you're a powder monkey. Will you serve the guns?"

"I'll not fire on innocent ships."

Behind him Tom erupted. "Just sign the bloody *Articles*!"

Dan folded his arms, his jaw set.

Calico Jack stared at the small, dark-haired lad in front of him. The boy's earnest, blue eyes never wavered.

157

"I like you, Master Sprat. You amuse me and I admire your spirit, but you've got to give me a reason to keep you, or the crew will throw you overboard. You have to understand that. They'll not carry a dead weight."

Dan said nothing.

The captain sighed and walked to the big stern window, staring out thoughtfully for a minute before turning back.

"You'll not fire on innocent ships, but not all ships are innocent." His slate-grey eyes bored into Dan. "Britain is at war with Spain. Would you fire on Spaniards?"

Dan considered this. "I suppose so. Yes."

"Well now we're getting somewhere." Calico Jack stroked his recently shaved chin and nodded slowly. "I'll take you on as a cabin boy — and part-time powder monkey whenever we can find some Spaniards for you to fight. And I'll see to it that you get all the dirty jobs on board. You understand if you'll not sign the *Articles* then you won't get a share of any plunder we take, and if we're caught they'll probably hang you anyway?"

"I'll take my chances, sir."

"There are no 'sirs' aboard *this* ship. You can call me Jack, or *Captain* if you prefer. George, show them around and explain their duties."

Calico Jack dismissed them and went back to the paperwork on his desk as the bosun led them out onto the rolling deck.

***

GLOSSARY

Admiralty	Body in charge of the Royal Navy.
Aft	Towards the stern of a ship.
Average Height	British sailors in 1720 were, on average, 5ft, 5ins tall (1.65m). Many were below 5 foot (1.52m).
Back Sails	To deliberately catch the wind in front of the sails to bring the ship to a halt.
Ballast	Heavy matter placed in a ship's hold to keep it steady when it has no cargo.
Bare Poles	A ship running without any sails up.
Barque	Three-masted ship with square-rigged sails, apart from the aftermost mast, which was fore and aft rigged.
Beat to Quarters	When a ship was about to go into action, drums would beat and the crew would run to their action stations.
Beau Nasty	A well-dressed but dirty person.
Belay	To make fast a rope by winding it round a belaying pin. It therefore came to mean, 'Hold fast', and was used in sailing slang as such. 'Belay there,' meant stop what you're doing.
Belaying Pin	Large wooden pin, placed in hole, mainly on the gunwales, used to fasten ropes to.
Bloody	Swearword. Short for 'By our Lady'.
Boarders	Sailors and marines who fought their way onto an enemy ship.
Bosun (Boatswain).	Warrant Officer who looks after the ship's boats, rigging and flags. Also usually in charge of every day discipline on board.
Bow	The pointy end of the ship.
Bowsprit	Large spar projecting over the bow.
Bow-chaser	Cannon in the bow. They pointed forwards, and were the only guns that could be fired if you were chasing a ship, hence the name.
Breeches	Pair of trousers cut off at the knee.
Brig	Sailing ship with two masts, both square-rigged.
Broadside	All the guns on one side of a warship and their simultaneous discharge.
Bulwark	Defensive railing around the deck of a ship.
Burgoo	Oatmeal boiled in water.
Canvas	Sails. These were made from canvas.

Captain's Daughter The Cat-o-nine-tails.

Cartridge A case containing the gunpowder charge for a gun.

Cast Off To let go a cable or rope securing a vessel to a buoy, wharf etc.

Cat-o-nine-tails Whip with nine knotted ropes attached to the handle.

Cat got your tongue? If a sailor got lippy with a ship's officer he would be flogged with the cat-o-nine-tails. The next time he passed him and there was no impertinent remark from the sailor, the officer would rub it in by asking, "What's the matter? Cat got your tongue?" This expression passed into the English language and is used if someone lippy is suddenly quiet after being told-off or punished in some way.

Not enough room to swing a **cat** This refers to swinging a cat-o-nine-tails, not one of the furry variety.

Let the cat out of the bag The whip was kept in a cloth bag (usually red to hide blood stains) to keep it from drying out. When you let the cat out of the bag then someone was in trouble. It eventually came to mean letting out a secret that would get someone in trouble.

Caulk Press tarred oakum, or other material, into the seams between the planks of a ship to prevent leaks.

Chain-shot Two solid cannonballs attached to each other by a length of chain. Designed to bring down a ship's masts and rigging.

Chasing Wind A wind coming from directly behind the ship.

Colours Flags.

Commodore Rank between captain and admiral.

Corny Faced Pimply.

Crow's Nest Lookout platform at the top of the mainmast.

Cudgel Short, thick stick used for fighting. Club. Cosh.

Cutlass Short, curved, broad-bladed sword used at sea.

Disrate To demote.

Double-Shotted A gun with 2 cannonballs in the barrel.

Farting Crackers Trousers.

Fife Small, military flute.

Flogging Whipping.

Foghorn A loud horn sounded by ships in fog so other vessels wouldn't collide with them.

Founder Sink.

Frigate	Fast two-deck warship with 30 to 60 cannons, often used for reconnaissance or to carry messages between ships-of-the-line.
Galley	The kitchen on a ship . Also a long, low-built vessel propelled by oars.
Grapeshot	Grape-sized metal pellets that would spread out and kill a large number of people when fired from a cannon at close range.
Gunport	A porthole for a gun. These were kept shut for safety except when the guns were to be fired.
Gunwale	Upper edge of a ship's side.
Gutfoundered	Hungry.
Halyard	A rope for hoisting a sail, yard or flag.
Hawser	Small cable or large rope.
Hawse Hole	A hole for a hawser to pass through.
Heads	The ships toilets. Basically holes in a plank set in the bows and dropping directly into the sea.
Headway	Forward motion of a ship.
Heave To	Bring a ship to a standstill using the wind.
Helmsman	The person steering the ship.
Hit the Deck	To drop suddenly to the ground. Originally a nautical term that became general usage.
Holystoning	The practice of cleaning a ship's decks by running heavy stones back and forth across them.
Hull Down	Where a ship's hull is hidden over the horizon and only the sails can be seen.
Idlers	Men who could sleep all night on board ship as they weren't assigned to any watch and, in theory, didn't have to work a night shift (e.g. Captain, Surgeon, Sailing Master, Purser, Bosun, and Gunner).
Jollyboat	A ship's smallest boat.
Keelhaul	Punishment where the victim has ropes tied to his arms and legs, and is pulled under the ship and back out the other side. This was normally done from side to side, but a particularly sadistic captain would have the man dragged from bow to stern, to increase the chance of him drowning.
Ladyhole	Small triangular space in the hold where the hull supported the rudder. It was well below the waterline and heavily timbered so it was the safest place on a ship during a battle. Any ladies on board were sent there for safety when action

stations were called, so it became known as the
'ladyhole'. (The term 'lady', and therefore the
ladyhole, did not extend to convicts, indentured
servants, or the wives of ordinary seamen).

Landlubber   A landsman or inexperienced sailor on board ship.
Landsman   A non-sailor.
Lanthorn   Obsolete spelling of 'lantern'.
Larboard   The left side of a ship. (From 'load board', the
                   side of the ship where you loaded and unloaded
                   goods). Now called 'port', as 'larboard' and
                   'starboard'sounded too alike and mistakes could
                   be made.
Larbowlines   Members of the larboard watch.
Launch   The largest of a warship's boats, used to ferry the
                   captain around.
League   Distance equal to about 3 nautical miles.
Learn the ropes People unused to ships had to literally 'learn the
                   ropes' as these controlled the sails as well as
                   raising the anchor and securing the ship to a dock.
                   It became common usage for learning anything
                   new.
Lee   Opposite side of the ship to where the wind blows.
Line Astern   A line of ships, each following the one in front.
Linstock   Stick holding a rope-match used to fire a gun.
Lobscouse   A salt meat stew with onions, potatoes and crushed
                   ship's biscuit. Popular in Liverpool, hence the
                   nickname, *Scousers*.
Loose Cannon   A gun that breaks loose from its moorings, which
                   has the potential to cause serious damage to the
                   ship and her crew. It has come to mean a
                   dangerously out of control person who can cause
                   damage to all around them.
Lubber Hole   Disparaging name for the hole at the bottom of
                   the crow's nest. Experienced sailors scorned to use
                   it and climbed in through the open top.
Magazine   Gunpowder storeroom.
Make Way   To move ahead.
Man-o-War   A warship.
Make and mend Before the times when uniforms were issued the
                   men made their own. When hands could be spared
                   from work, the call was 'make and mend clothes.'
Masthead   The top of the mast.
Mast-heading   Punishment where someone was forced to stay at

	the top of the mainmast for a period of time.
Matelot	Ordinary seaman below the rank of officer.
Midshipman	Rank in the Royal Navy, above naval cadet and below sub-lieutenant. Usually teenagers.
Mizzenmast	The aft sail on a two-masted vessel.
Muck Spout	Foul mouthed person.
Navy List	Official list of all the officers in the Royal Navy and Marines.
Oakum	Loose fibre, got by unpicking old tarry ropes, used for caulking seams of ships.
Pike	Weapon consisting of a long, wooden shaft with a flat, pointed steel tip. (Similar to a spear).
Pipe Down	Be quiet. The expression comes from 'pipe down hammocks' when bosun's mates would blow their pipes to tell the crew to fetch their hammocks and go below to sleep.
Pissdales	Urinals by a ship's rails.
Pitch	Where a ship plunges so that the bow and stern rise and fall alternately.
Powder Monkey	Boy whose job was to keep the ship's cannons supplied with gunpowder.
Prayer Book	Small holystone used to clean corners of the deck.
Press-gang	Body of men used to obtain recruits to the Royal Navy by force.
Pressed Man	Someone recruited by a press-gang.
Rake	To fire a broadside into the stern or bow of an enemy ship. The cannonballs would travel the length of the ship causing terrible destruction.
Ramrod	Rod for ramming the charge down a muzzle-loading gun.
Ratlines	Small rope lines fastened across a sailing ship's shrouds like the rungs of a ladder, used for climbing the rigging.
Rigging	System of ropes and tackle for supporting masts and controlling sails.
Roll	Where a ship sways from side to side.
Round-shot	Solid iron cannonballs.
Sailing close to the wind	Sailing into the wind as near to directly as a sailboat can. This was dangerous in square-riggers because if the wind came round to blow in the front of the sails instead of behind, then they could be 'taken aback'. As this was dangerous it became a saying that someone was, 'sailing close

	to the wind' if they were living dangerously.
Scuppers	Channels running alongside the bulwarks of a ship to drain water from the deck and out through the scupper-holes back to the sea.
Sheet	Rope attached to the lower lee corner of a sail to extend it into the wind. (It can also refer to the sail itself). The sheet is the line that controls the sails. If the line is not secured, the sail flops in the wind, and the ship loses headway and control. If three sails are loose, the ship is out of control. so, if a man was drunk, they'd say he was *three sheets to the wind*.
Ship's Biscuit	Biscuits that were double-baked to make them last longer for ship's voyages. The problem was that it made them difficult to bite into.
Ship's Log	Official diary kept by the captain.
Ship-of-the-line	Warship large enough to stand in line with the rest of the main battleships and exchange broadsides with the enemy.
Skiff	Small rowing boat.
Spindrift	Spray blown from the crests of waves.
Starboard	The right side of a ship. This is were the *steer board* used to be before rudders were invented.
Starbowlines	Members of the starboard watch.
Start	To beat a sailor with a knotted rope. A casual punishment applied mainly by bosuns, without trial or a hearing in front of an officer.
Stern	The back part of a ship.
Stern-chaser	As with 'bow-chaser' but sited in the stern to fire at pursuing (chasing) vessels.
Strike (the colours)	To pull down the flag and surrender the ship.
Studding Sail	A small extra sail put up in a light wind or when trying to sail as fast as possible.
Tack	Sailing ships could not sail directly into the wind. To make way in the direction of the wind they therefore had to sail at an angle to it on one tack, then switch to a opposite tack, slowly zigzagging into the general direction of the wind.
Taken Aback	Where sailing ships were sailing close to the wind, if the wind came round to blow in the front of the sails instead of behind, then they could be 'taken aback'. i.e. the sails would be pushing in the opposite direction to the ship's momentum and it

could shudder to a stop or lose its sails or masts. This led to the saying, 'taken aback' when applied to people metaphorically.

Take the wind from their sails To sail close to windward of a ship so your sails catch the wind and block it from reaching theirs, so you can overtake them or outmanoeuvre them. It now means to deflate someone.

Tars (Jack Tars)   Royal Navy sailors. They were called tars because their hands were always covered with the tar used to waterproof the ship's ropes. They also used it to braid their pigtails and to waterproof their hats and trousers. Basically, they stank of tar.

Thirty-two Pounder Gun that fired a cannonball weighing thirty-two pounds (15.4 kg).

Topmen   The most agile and experienced sailors who would climb highest in the rigging to furl and unfurl the topsails etc. They were higher paid than the waisters who stayed on deck in the waist of the ship.

Touch-hole   Hole at the top rear of a cannon through which the gunpowder was ignited.

Tow rag   A rag tied to the end of a rope, towed along in the water then pulled up when someone needed to wipe their bum.

True Colours   Ships used to fly false flags to bamboozle their enemies. So to show your true colours meant to reveal your true identity.

Waister   Landsman or inexperienced seaman with no sailing skills. They were kept in the middle (the waist) of the ship where they'd do menial tasks where no particular skill was needed. This is where the modern term, waster', came from, not from 'waste' as is commonly thought.

Watch   a) Those members of a ship's crew who are on duty at the same time.
b) One of the seven divisions of the working day on board ship.

Weathergage   Upwind of another ship. (Where you want to be in a chase or a battle).

Weather Rail   The rail on the quarterdeck facing the wind. The captain would patrol this half of the quarterdeck and no-one could enter it without his permission.

Went About	Turned into the wind onto an opposite tack.
Windward	The side of the ship the wind blows on.
Yard	A long beam for spreading sails on.
Yardarm	The end of the yard.

If you enjoyed this book then please take a minute to leave an honest review at:

AMAZON.CO.UK
BEFORE THE MAST: The Adventures of Dan Leake
J.R. MULHOLLAND
amazon.co.uk/dp/B08T6JY36M

Keep your eye out for the other two books in the trilogy, *Hoist the Black Flag* and *The Pirate Republic*.

Thanks for reading.

J.R. Mulholland

Printed in Great Britain
by Amazon